I0456882

END OF TIMES BOOK 1

NAMELESS SOLDIERS

E.N. Clay

Copyright © 2019 E.N. Clay

All rights reserved.

Glossary included in the end.

Publisher

Den Väntades Vänner

info@dvv.se

www.dvv.se

First edition published 2019-02-11

ISBN 978-91-86267-23-0

My God,

who can have tasted the sweetness of Your love,

then wanted another in place of You?

The Whispered Prayer of the Lovers

To Imam Hossein, the greatest martyr of all times.

To SSH, whom I owe my soul.

To Haji, for never losing faith in us.

We will show them Our signs in the horizons and within themselves until it becomes clear to them that it is the truth.

The Holy Qur'an 41:53

1

There are massive tornados descending from the dark sky. Compact, flashing like lightning, but they are neither lightning nor tornados. Angels, they are angels. Coming down one after the other. I breath out, "It's the angels that descend upon earth for zohoor, the end of times." I pull up my phone, start Slack, NSI's internal chat app, and write, "Look out @channel."

I woke up, shaken and sweaty. This was the second time in a month that I had dreamt of the end of times. I looked out the window. Fajr, the dawn prayer, was closing in.

"You are the Dark Forces," roared Laqis. "And I am your commander, by birth right and by rank, appointed by my grandfather himself."

"All hail Azazel!" chanted the special unit of *djinn*, the invisible species created from smokeless fire.

"I had a vision tonight," Laqis continued. "In it I saw the coming of the End of Times. Angels descending and scattered believers from the descendents of Adam trying to mobilize. They are no match to us. We will crush them as we have always crushed them since our Master was cast out of Paradise!"

"We will use the same tactics as our Master did,

divide and conquer, turning the sons of Adam against each other!" said one of the demons.

"Indeed we will," Laqis said. "By inciting Cain to slay Abel our Master laid the foundation for the Dark Forces. Our mission is higher levels of human chaos and our weapon is manipulation. By proving how weak and feeble the tribe of Adam is, we can restore the honor of our Master in the Divine Realms and demonstrate to God Himself that *He* was wrong; Adam, that mischievous being, should have been the one to submit to Azazel!"

As I sat in my bed trying to orient myself in the dark room I was overcome by a sudden realization that sent shivers down by spine. If the angels are descending for the end of times, it also means the djinns are assembling. The prophecies stated that Iblis, the outcast, *the* Satan, will be beheaded at the final fight, and with no doubt, the djinn will try to prevent that from happening. Unfortunately, the amount of information about them and their tactics were scarce among the books. There were bits and pieces scattered, but I had yet to cross roads with an author who had exposed them thoroughly in a systematic matter. I knew they were experts of manipulation who used people with power and influence such as politicans, actors and musicians, to execute their schemes. And if someone didn't comply, they'd lose *everything*. On a piece of writing I had found on the dark net, the author, who was anonymous but who clearly had insight into matters, considering all the sensitive information he wrote about, said that there was a group among the satans, appointed by Lucifer himself, who were the masterminds of all conspiracies going on. They called themselves the Dark Forces. Although it may seem odd, fashion and music trends were usually initiated by the Dark Forces. They used mental weapons, such as whispers - infiltrating minds, persuading weak people to execute their plans. Hollywood was also operated by them with these methods. They also controlled most politicians by inciting their primitive desires, playing them against each other with hearsay. And this is where the media, unknowingly, played a crucial role. A fledgling young reporter could be lured into fighting for the greater good by exposing corrupt politicians, forgetting the 18th paragraph of The Art of War: "All warfare is based on deception". However, a warrior of light knows the exact moment of attack by measuring the overall impact of the war at a whole. Therefore exposing a corrupt politician, or even overthrowing an entire regime at a certain moment could pave the way for more corruption. We saw it when Afghanistan and Iraq were invaded after nine-eleven, with the Arabic spring tailing shortly after and the closing finale of Syria's civil war and the assault on Yemen, setting the world on a horrendous fire.

We haven't had any direct encounter with the Dark Forces yet, NSI were insignificant to them, but I knew it would happen sooner or later. I got out of the bed and stood facing the bathroom mirror. I looked hard at my own reflection, thinking, *Who am I? How much longer will I be a short sighted donkey, seeing only the grass by my feet, stubborn, or perhaps afraid, to look past the grazing fields, up towards the endless sky? When will I become the real human whom I was designated to be? When will I manifest God's command through me and bend nature by my sheer willpower?* I sighed and proceeded with doing *wudho*, the ritual washing for prayers. I washed my face, *"brighten my face on the day when all faces are darkened of sorrow"*, I thought. I washed my right arm, *"give me my sword in my right hand"*, stroking my hair, *"shower Your mercy upon me"*. And finally I stroked my feet with my wet hands, *"and don't let my feet slip on* sirat, *the straight bridge"*.

After prayers I decided against going back to sleep, instead I prepared for school. The dream had made me hungry. My stomach roared after its *sunnah* bowl. *I should make a YouTube video of the recipe,* I thought as I poured flakes in the bowl, bit seven dates into four pieces each and added them to my flakes, poured honey over the spectacle and finished off with wheat milk. *Et voila, done in three minutes, Jamie Oliver should feature it in his 30-Minute Meals show,* I said to myself. I started with *Bismillah,* took my first bite and thought of the exactness in Prophet Mohammad's teachings, that seven dates a day helped the body and soul, increased the energy level, boosted the sexual drive and gave spiritual protection throughout the day. I took my bowl and sat by the computer looking through my news list. There is a special feeling when you build something yourself, customized for your own needs. Some people paint, others do carpentry and renovate their homes. I coded my own system for highly efficient news reading. It consisted of several selected minimal news feed. Basically, I went through a personal list of news sources, picking out articles according to a preset template of keywords I'd chosen; all pertaining what could have to do with zohoor, connected to signs for the end of times, that I`d read about in various religious litterature. Some articles were color-marked after relevance; red meant top relevance and yellow was medium to high relevance. The news feed displayed title, source, thumbnail, the first paragraph of the article and a "read more" link. It's also unified, but with filtering capabilities.

Accordingly I could quickly get updated with the latest mainstream news everyone's reading, without wasting much time searching or getting distracted by click bates and celebrity gossip that lurked around in the online newspapers. I evaded everything that smelled like it could be orchestrated by the Dark Forces. Going through the mainstream news usually took about ten minutes, the same time I needed to finish my *sunnah* bowl.

Also, I'd created a similar feed with alternate news sources. And a third one with underground forums, bulletin boards, obscure subreddits and shady online societies that I liked to keep an eye on. All these shortened news items were also stored in my database and with one simple click I could tell the system to fetch the news article and store it in its entirety, of course as bare boned text without ads and images. So, it was super easy for me to reference articles and news when needed. And finally, there was a feed with all private messages, comment threads and discussions I am involved with throughout the Internet. I didn't need to actually surf into Facebook and get hit with a storm of profile-targeted ads or, once again, get distracted by click baits and be tempted into liking or re-sharing others' posts which aggregated an online profile of me, that was then sold to advertisement networks. And one day, when I am a "person of interest" that same data will be in my journal for some government agent to analyze. So I pay for a top level VPN and proxy service, used by the pirate community for file sharing, to hide my online presence. And with my own news platform I could stay out of the online mess and read just exactly what I need to read or get engaged in. Posts I write, I write from my platform, so I always have a local copy saved with timestamp, source link and whatever I'm replying to. The reason for always backing up what I wrote was two folded; access to what was written in case the online version disappeared (it had happened several times that a user deleted a post for whatever reason, but now I could have my *own* profile database of every user I engaged with), searchability and also, re-usability. I'd noticed that discussions, questions and comments usually recurred so I'd learnt to word my posts in a generic matter so that I could easily search, find and re-post them every time a topic arouse. I'd named my system *e-jihad*, electronic resistance, because that is precisely what it was. E-jihad rested on a little neat Raspberry Pi that I had hidden away back home. It's accessed through SSH, a secure tunnel for establishing a connection. And, I had coded the Raspberry with specific public keys that were allowed to establishing a connection. Hence everyone else were denied access even before the login prompt would be shown. In case of fire, or worse, police raid, I had configured the Raspberry to take a nightly copy of entire e-jihad, including the database, encrypt it and upload it to the cloud. I had selected a host in Russia for my backups so it wouldn't look too suspicious (as compared to a host in Iran for example) while still not being subject to US raiding laws. All in all, I had a neat little setup that I was rather proud of.

When I had gone through my entire e-jihad feed and taken all needed actions in my stream I went out to catch the train to LTH, Lund's Technical University, one of Sweden's finest. I was in my second year of computer sciences and even though I was good at it, I was getting bored with all lame exercises that needed to be done in order to graduate. Sure you learnt the basics and fundamentals of programming and electronics but the raw content wasn't exactly cutting edge technology. I had already learnt hardware close C programming and object oriented Java targeting mobile development on my own following MIT courses on iTunes University, as well as some electronics and soldering when I experimented with my Arduinos and Raspberrys at home. Today was no different. Professor Nyberg was going through different sorting algorithms that I'd already read about while investigating Google's ability to search through enormous amounts of data and still present an accurate result list within half a second. I was getting bored and sleepy when my phone silently vibrated. A push notification from e-jihad. It was set to notify me when "breaking news" articles were released. It read, "Long sought university hacker Stakkato has been arrested by Swedish police". For a split second the world stood still; I could only hear my heart beat faster and faster. This meant time was running out. I needed to act before I missed the boat. I fired up Slack and wrote to Mohsen Hajizadeh aka Haji with capital H, my mentor and NSI's group leader, "Stakkato has been arrested, we need to extract the Griffin now or forget about the whole thing. What do you think?"

"Do it," he replied immediately. Haji was a man of instant action, in mystic Sufi terms a "son of the moment". He never hesitated, fearless and always head first into battle.

2

Stakkato, or as I knew him, Philip Johansson, was a sixteen year old kid that started hacking when he was only ten years old. My neighbor back in the day. As a three year older more experienced computer geek, I helped him set up his first personal computer, his sixth birthday gift. He found it more fascinating to crack games than playing them. Two years later he learnt the basics of Python and programmed a simple role-playing app which was lauded by the kids in the neighbourhood. It was when he, all by himself, found a bug in Windows 7 that allowed him to change the desktop wallpaper of any user in the domain, that he became thrilled by hacking into systems. All pupils had laughed hysterically in computer class when their teacher logged in and, to his terror, saw his desktop wallpaper featuring a bare-breasted woman with a tomato in her mouth. Similar to the Apple logo, the tomato was chewn. And to the right was written, "STAKKATO OWNZ U!" But that wasn't the end of it. Philip had recorded the entire happening and sent the video to FailArmy, who broadcasted it to all their thirteen million YouTube followers. That might sound evil but at his core, Philip was doing what he thought was right. His best friend had confined to him that the same teacher once had made a discreet sexual move, caressing him on his back while bending over his desk to help with a assignment, and the fingers had gone all the way down. Philip's desktop hack made that teacher both lose his reputation, and later quit his job as he was never again taken seriously again by students.

That was when Philip's career as the notorious hacker "Stakkato" began. His technical setup was smart from a juridical point of view. His home server was configured as a connection hub, so hackers he trusted were granted access as passthrough to other nodes, before ending up on a targeted host. Stakkato's mother was a doctor. Once, he joined her to work and while waiting for her in the research lab, he found a forgotten post-it sign with login information to Monolith; one of Sweden's largest super computers, located in Linköping University. Monolith was used by scientists to query complex calculations needed for their research. Stakkato went through seven VPN nodes, Virtual Private Networks; a secure tunnel between two computers with all exchanged data traffic being encrypted, before connecting to Monolith. On Monolith, he then replaced the login service with a service of his own. It did the exact same thing with one important difference, whatever the user wrote in the login prompt was also saved and uploaded to a private server of his own. Some users on Monolith connect to other super computers in Sweden. Even around the globe to the Israel's Technion University, across the Atlantic to John Hopkins University in Baltimore in northeast USA and to the southwest, the location of San Diego's "Data Star". All logins are saved and where within Stakkato's reach as well as all his trusted friends who have access to his home connection hub. And I am one of them.

So, Stakkato being detained meant that the police most likely had made a razzia and grabbed all his servers. But luckily, I've copied a few gems among all thousands of logins stored on his server. It would take the police a couple of weeks at tops to go through all those gigabytes of sensitive data and alert relevant parties that their system have been breached. I gave myself one week to execute *Operation Griffin*.

Amids Stakkato's gigantic text files were eight spectacular lines of vital information that I had stumbled upon a couple of months earlier. I don't think even Stakkato himself, or anyone else in his trusted company, had discovered these eight lines. The lines contained the IP address to Patuxent River Naval Air Systems command, followed by *root*. And then: the password. Root was the super user of any Unix system. It has the freedom and rights to do *anything* it wants on the system. And here comes the juicy part: Patuxent River is the headquarters for the American Air Force, responsible for holding the US Marine fighter jets in top shape. Operation Griffin was simple but deadly if executed with precision and a big amount of luck, or *tawfiq* - God's granting of success - depending on how you looked at it. My plan was to discreetly hack Patuxent River, extract whatever classified documents that are stored and forward them to the head of *The Axis of Resistance* - Iran. When I discovered the login to Patuxent River on Stakkato's files I'd deliberately not erased them on Stakkato's server after having copied them to my own. I thought *if* the police somehow manages to disclose his identity and raid his house, they will eventually find the login and alert the US agencies. They will also know that Stakkato's server was a connection hub; thus if there is a hack against Patuxent, it could be anyone of the dussins of unknown hacker aliases that had access to his server.

Extracting the classified documents was one thing, to deliver them to trustful hands within Iran was a whole other. Iran was a cluster of bureaucracy, all with powerful long claws and personal agendas. And all of them masked themselves behind the banner of *zohoor* and the coming of Imam Mahdi. This is where Haji played a critical role. It was his mission to identify whoever was of some high caliber and influence on one hand and trustworthy, working for the same cause, on the other.

As the teacher was drawing search algorithm schemes on the whiteboard I drew my own schemes in my notebook. I planned my attack to be at 4 a.m., the same night. The time would be 9 p.m. in Patuxent River, so the security surveillance team and IT admins would've ended their shift. In my mind, I was already simulating how to execute Operation Griffin when my phone buzzed again. *"New post in Poetical Battle"*. The entire mental picture of my master plan vanished like smoke beside a rotating fan. I looked out the window and observed how the branches were swaying back and forth at the mercy of the wind. Firmly grounded, yet movable, while we lose our feet at the smallest gust.

> *What she seek lays in the breeze of tornados*
> *enchanted by your vivid motion*
> *lips twinned together…tasting unseen wonders*
> *settle the desert storm, blindfolding your way*
> *ride the wind of Salomon to arrive at Heaven's*
> *bay*

This passion arouse her to a wave on your ocean
dropping her heart in your pond....slowly circles
spread abroad
reed whisper to spirits.....feel this love ode
She sing words of Moses unto the sea
arise, embrace......wash me in thee

I felt a shiver down my spine as I was reading her poetic lines. There was such a passion in her words, they were touching, no *enchanting*. MuslimChat was one of the online forums I frequented. It was a rather large online community with over 10'000 members, but it was dominated with dogmatic beliefs that colored the discussions, usually of religious or political topics. Over the years I'd gained a good reputation by writing factual posts, stripped of emotions and rhetorics, and backed up with solid references. I didn't just post a *fatwa*, a religious decree, when a member posted a *fiqh* question. I also provided the exact link to each answer so that anyone could double check. Same went for all religious topics - references to Qur'an verses, hadiths, research from scholars and the like. It was within my reach using my e-jihad platform and smart Google searches. When I became known as a knowledgeable and respectable member, I started revolutionizing; blowing away dogma with soul and vision. I did a series of write ups on *irfan*, Islam's spiritual and mystical dimensions, and then I slowly started posting poems. All *urefa*, Islamic mystics, wrote, or rather, *outpoured* poetry. They assumed the role of a loving seeing father who wants to describe the beautiful landscape during sunset for his blind son. Traditional words fall short when depicting the scenery and this is where poetry come to rescue. It's like juice, concentrated with meaning and insight. At first I posted poems by *ulema*, Islamic scholars, to show that this art was indeed practiced by them. Then I posted a few of my own, and finally I started the poetical battle where I challenged several other members to write poetry. Kind of like a snowfall effect, all of a sudden a dozen of unpolished rubies, free-minded, who saw things from another light, emerged from the thousand.

But her words, Layla's, were something else, something *otherworldly*. I didn't read her words, I *felt* them. Only a few other authors had such an instant effect on me, their words caressed me. I read the opening line to her verse repeatedly, *"What she seek lays in the breeze of tornados"*. She couldn't have known about my dream, how could she? Still, that line awoke something deep within; a sleeping storm, clawing itself out. I felt the urge to write something back, right away, I needed to...

delve into her mind.

Light split asunder
Tornados of angel wings
Fall in love with him

I re-read my haiku a couple of times and finally posted it. Class was already over and I hadn't heard a word of what Professor Nyberg had said about conventional database algorithms. I grabbed my backpack and hit the hallway to the dining room to grab a lunch. Getting up at the crack of dawn had left me famished. I hurried to fill my stomach. I couldn't help but notice the *shalwar-qamis*, wildy bearded South Asian gang, focusing on a female student. Her black tights, boots, miniskirt, slim red cardigan and night dark scarf, left no questions to her edginess. My focus shifted back to beard-gang as they mumbled,"Look what she's wearing! Isn't she ashamed of herself?", loud enough for her and me, standing a few feet away, to hear. *Shame*, I thought, instinctively clenching my fist. Seven years of martial arts had left its traces. "Hey!", I shouted. "There no shame in being dressed. It is, however, a shame to undress someone in your mind."

"What did you say?!", one of the tougher guys mouthed, stepping in front of me. I concluded him to be the alpha in their pack.

"You heard me," I said, taking a step forward, almost touching him with my nose. I was completely calm. But he was agitated, and I sensed a discomfort in his sight. There was a moment of silence, then one of the teachers rushed forth and pulled me back. "I am Farooq, remember my name," he said as they all walked away. I knew I had to deal with them again, sooner or later. *Hasbunallah wa n'emal wakil - God is sufficient and the best advocate*, I thought. When everyone had scattered the girl from the scene approached me and said, "Thank you. No one's ever done that for me." Her eyes where wide open without any shyness yet they radiated some sort of restrained curiosity.

"No need to thank me," I said. "There is nothing I dislike more than the Haram Police. Well nothing more than perhaps those intellectuals who fuel these shallow people." *Gosh, why did I say that?! I don't want to scare her away by dry politics.*

She chuckled. "The Haram Police?! Haven't heard that one before. So I guess you are a Muslim too?"

I grinned, relieved that she hadn't paid attention to the political part. "Yes, isn't that obvious? Perhaps you missed the beard, the dark hair, the brown eyes and," I turned around so she could see my backpack pin.

"313? Well isn't that ironic! I was saved from the Taliban Squad by an apocalyptic *mujahed*!"

She laughed, and so did I. She was both easy and fun to talk with, but it felt awkward standing in the corridor with all bypasses.

"Wanna grab lunch before the end of times?", I asked kindly.

"Yes," she beamed. "Oh and I'm Nora."

"I'm Ali."

3

I found her green eyes captivating. They were like sparkling emeralds just beneath the surface of a dark ocean. She was eating a crispy sallad. "Why are your eyes green?" I said.

She smirked. "Because my father is The Hulk," she teased and took a demonstrative bite of the sallad.

I grabbed the glass of soda, whirled it around as I caressed my beard with the other hand and examined her. "Hmm, so that make you the She-Hulk then?"

"Indeed it does, detective. You don't want to upset me," she declared.

She leaned her head against the back of her hand.

"So why didn't you unleash your Hulk powers on the Haram Police then?" I challenged her.

"Well, I was about to, but then *you* came in and ruined the show, so I got distracted," she said, pointing at me with her lipstick-shaped finger.

"*I* distracted *you*?" I exclaimed hinting at her with my finger and forgetting to close my mouth in bafflement.

"Ok, let's put down our guns before anyone gets shot." She made a show of blowing her finger and putting it down and smiled at me. I liked it.

"What's up with the 313?" She positioned herself

upright again, studying my backpack.

"Don't you believe in it?" I followed her eyes search.

"In what?" She met my eyes.

"A savior that will come when the earth has reached the final stage of injustice and corruption, cleansing it all and establish a divine just government. The Buddists think it's Buddha, the Jews think it's a descendant of David, the Christians think it's Jesus and we Muslims believe it's the Mahdi, *Imam* Mahdi, accompanied by Jesus."

"I guess so. Well, I haven't thought of it much. Just heard the name once or twice. I haven't really understood the connection to 313 though, what does it stand for?"

"Imam Mahdi will have 313 governors that answer directly to him. They will be spread out around the world and govern according to his rule."

"Oh," she murmured. "And you think you can be one of them?"

"Perhaps not a governor but some sort of deputy at least. I mean, ruling over Malmö region or perhaps county Skåne wouldn't be so bad."

She chuckled. "If you try to rule over me, I will definitely become the She-Hulk."

"I am Batman. I will outwit your rage," I

snapped.

She chuckled again. She got the comic reference. I liked *that* a lot.

"So where are you from?" she asked.

"I am from Khorasan, northeast of Iran. I am from Ilam in the western border of Iran-Iraq. I am from a small village two hours from the border. And I am the son of both capitals, Tehran and Baghdad." I looked at her.

"Wow, how fascinating! So you are Iranian and Iraqi?" She crossed her legs.

I cleared my throat. "And Kurdish."

"Oh."

"What? You sound Turkish," I joked, trying to meet one prejudice with another.

"I am," she said.

A moment of awkward silence.

"I didn't know there are Turkish She-Hulks." I leaned back in the chair.

"I didn't know there are Iranian Batmans."

"Actually there is," I moved forth, fixing my eyes on her. "He is called Behrooz Ein instead of Bruce Wayne."

"What?! Don't tell me you have an Iranian Bruce Lee as well?!" She burst out into laughter.

"We do," I said. "He is called Behrooz Ali, of course."

"Ok Mr. Behrooz, so what do you study?" she

grimaced.

"Computer engineering," I said.

"Ooo, a hacker!"

She has no idea, I thought. "What about you?"

"Social studies."

She looked at my empty plate. "Coffee?"

"I'd love that!" I admired her stature as she walked away.

The lunch break was long over, but our talk wasn't. We spoke of many things, yet it felt as if we had only scratched the surface. There was more depth to her than I had first anticipated. I enjoyed talking to her. Perhaps because I finally had met someone who had touched me. Someone who I could connect to, who had common grounds with me. Which is rare, with me feeling like an outsider, or even *stranger*, in school. Beverages and parties were the only topics my schoolmates ever bothered with. Me, as the only child to my parents and a foreigner in all my classes, since kindergarten, sought connections in the online societies. I found shady, underground, hacker clubs. I shut up and absorbed whatever the seniors said. Frequent topics of debate were freedom of information, sharing and spreading and the pirate culture and its conflict with the corporate propertarianism that dominated the world. When mainstream media finally came onboard the debate, that is when The

Pirate Bay trial began, the leet had already moved on. They had already anticipated the outcome of the trial and were now concerned with the next step: how to guarantee the free exchange of information without compromising your integrity. How? With encryption. I observed how they cooperated in building a secure platform. Later on, WikiLeaks relied upon it for informants to safely transfer sensitive data.

I felt at home in those hacker forums, but I still felt somewhat outside. They were sharp-witted, and the logic that their code was built by, also dominated their speech and way of reasoning. In all but one question, *the* question. Who had created the universe? They discarded religion, often mockingly. I didn't say much, but I found that logical flaw disturbing. There was either no First Cause that purposely initiated the creation, or there was - that's at least a fifty percent probability - so how can they discard it so simply? I found it particularly contradictive how they could build up a world, based on cause and effect, depend their lives upon it, but that chain of causes mysteriously vanished when it came to the First Cause? I mean, come on! There was one simple *truth* to all of it: acknowledging a First Cause meant there was a Creator; who had an aim with everything's creation. Life has a purpose, it wasn't random, it was *intended*. And with that intention came responsibility, and an afterlife. And with that responsibility came restrictions. Our bodies, our souls, our very existence, are loans entrusted to us. Loans to be returned. We don't own our bodies, so we aren't at liberty to do as we wish with them.

> Indeed, we offered the Trust to the heavens and the earth and the mountains, and they declined to bear it and feared it; but man [undertook to] bear it. Indeed, he was unjust and ignorant. (Qur'an 33:72)

What was this trust but my life? My body? My soul? My very existence that I am assigned to safeguard and blossom? I was only eleven, so I couldn't really express it in words, but I felt a hole for the whole. There was a passion in me that didn't long for anything, from another human being. That was until I stumbled upon Maolavi Rumi's famous opening verses to his "Mathnawi":

> *Listen to the story told by the reed,*
> *of being separated.*
>
> *"Since I was cut from the reedbed,*
> *I have made this crying sound.*

Anyone apart from someone he loves
understands what I say.

Anyone pulled from a source
longs to go back.

At any gathering I am there,
mingling in the laughing and grieving,

a friend to each, but few
will hear the secrets hidden"

His words struck me and deeply touched me. "Anyone pulled from the source longs to go back". What was the source that I yearned for? How could Maolavi depict my feelings so strikingly in his poem, both unmanteled the reason and the *way*? That winter I told my father, who was a devout man but who kept his faith to himself, not bothering me and mom with it, "Dad please buy me a Qur'an, in Swedish, I want to discover my origin."

We bought a copy from the local mosque. We were ironically overcharged a hundred kronas, compared to the price in the local bookshop. Anyhow, I devoured the Qur'an in a month, kept asking questions, kept searching online for more. My thirst to understand intensified. In that wave of learning, I had an unexpected dream. Before that, I hadn't dreamt since the age of five or six. Back then, my dreams consisted of crawling worms, spiders and insects. But this one was different, it was *real*. I saw a fire emerging in Tunis, then spreading all over the Middle East, burning down Egypt and Libya, then reaching Syria, where it escalated from earth, meeting the sky's thunders. There were tanks and soldiers of different colors on the ground, the sky was filled with fighter jets. It was complete chaos, and from this chaos waves upon waves of people were running and screaming, "The End of Times is happening!"

I had awoken, restless and confused. My heart was pounding anxiously. I noticed my shirt was drained in sweat. I called my dad at work and narrated the dream. "InshaAllah it's a good sign, don't be afraid son," he said reassuringly. I didn't think of it much more after that, instead I concentrated on learning prayers. Two weeks later, the 18th of December 2010, I came home after the last day at school, to start my Christmas holidays, watching some TV. I'd turned on the television and was completely stunned. Bouazizi had set himself on fire and had become the catalyst for the Tunisian Revolution. And as such, the Arab spring was kindled. What terrified me was the fact that I'd witnessed those same scenes two weeks earlier, in my dream. With the events spreading and unfolding in neighbor countries, I recognized each happening, one after the other. That Christmas holidays my dad spent the equivalent cost of a Playstation 3 in buying books for me, twenty in totalt, ranging from Islamic history, fundamentals of faith, hadith collections to more heavy philosophical works. My mom gifted me a translator pen for Christmas (it was important for her to commemorate Christmas to some degree, to feel assimilated), so I could just swipe over a word and it would provide the Swedish translation on the display. Really *handy*. When I started the next term in January I had read more then half of them.

I snapped back to reality, Nora was observing me.

"Black, white or sweet?"

"Umm, white *and* sweet," I murmured. "So what do you want to do when you graduate?"

"I want to be a voice for the silent victims," she stated.

I raised my eyebrows. "Silent victims?"

"Yes," she said. "Have you ever met someone who has felt excruciating physical pain or mental agony or the torture of waiting in suspense for the 'next time'? And they have not one person to vocal their hurt to. The kind of oppression that makes one lose faith in God, or at least not understand His wisdom." She sighed and observed my face as I absorbed the question. "I want to be a voice for *that* soul. Not just another psychologist or school welfare officer that listens and invoices and goes on with her life. I want to be the one who accompanies them through the whole process, the one to actually put an end to their oppression. If it's an abused child in a broken family, I wouldn't just hand them over to a foster family; the ones who live off a bunch of foster kids, like the social services do. As if that would end their hardships." I noticed how her words affected herself. The tone was sharper and her cheeks became slightly red as if a fire was burning her from the inside. She felt very familiar with the subject. "Instead, I'd want to *connect* them to a loving, caring family. I'd want to establish trust, link people."

As she spoke, I thought of Imam Hossein's words, *Don't oppress the one who has none but God.* "Have you met any silent victim yourself?" I asked.

Nora looked at me with heavy eyes, "Yes," she said. "Marie. A couple of years ago, when all those refugees started pouring in, I volunteered in a refugee camp downtown. And that's where I met her. She was a teenager like me, from West Africa, and she knew English. We kind of bonded. She was beautiful but very shy, almost afraid. I could see, in her dark eyes, that something was broken inside." Nora paused and looked out the window. "Even though she was a refugee she helped me in the kitchen. Sometimes she would come over to my house just to hang out and be a normal teenager for a while. But still it didn't take long for her joy to be overshadowed with that inner grief. And finally, she opened up and told me her story."

I looked at her, holding the tip of my beard with my fingers. "What did she say, if I may ask?"

"It's pretty dark, are you sure you want to hear it?", she cautioned.

"Tell me," I reassured.

"Well, Marie and her friends where outside when they met a patrol of five heavily armed rebels. They kidnaped them and took them to some rebel house in the outskirts of their city. Later, the gang came and separated Marie from her friend, leaving her alone in a small, suffocating room. And shortly after that, four well-built men in their thirties joined her. They told her to undress. She refused, telling them she's a virgin, that it's not right in the eyes of God to rape virgins. She begged them, telling them that she'd live under the shadow of it her entire life, would they do it." Nora's eyes started watering, and I braced myself to what she said next. "One of them slapped her hard on the face while the others hit her with their guns. They told her to shut up, that they didn't care, that they've raped so many and that she wouldn't be an exception. One of them suggested to strip her naked and put her under a firing squad. She cried her eyes out, frightened and praying for help." Nora sighed. I could hear the hurt in her voice. "They started ripping off her clothes, and one of them audaciously bit her back. She still has the mark of it. She was then pushed down to the ground. They got sick of her crying so one of them slapped her and tied her mouth with a rag. She could hardly breathe. Then the biggest one of them forced open her legs and raped her. The four of them spent two hours with her and each raped her at least twice. She felt disgusted, disconnected from her own body, shame and pain filled her." Tears ran down her cheek, as if she was in the same room with Marie. "She bleeded heavily and when they finally undid her mouth she begged them to let her go. They insulted her and said they'd have her until each and every one of them was satisfied. She spent three days in that house."

I realized I was biting the backside of my index finger as the words sunk in. Nora was sobbing.

After a while I broke the silence. "What did you do?"

She wiped away her tears with the back of her

sleeve, "I found a support group for raped women," she said. "I took Marie there. Later on, Human Rights Watch published her story and she's granted permanent residence permit. She was a talented sewer so I made a deal with her: I would buy her a sewing-machine and help her start up a business, on the condition that when she'd start getting profitable, she'd do the same for another silent victim. She said I was crazy to think she'd succeed, but she made the deal." A little smile broke the dark clouds. "I bought her a sewing-machine, asked a Turkish friend of mine, who owned a clothing store, if Marie could have a corner to display her clothes, then I opened an Instagram account for her and promoted her online."

"What happened then?" I asked eagerly, not noticing that my eyes were wet. "Did she succeed?"

"Well, she is a co-owner of the store now and she took in an apprentice to fulfill her part of our contract."

"SobhanAllah! That's so amazing!" I exclaimed.

"Yes." We looked at each other, our faces beamed with relief.

"I truly believe you will accomplish your goals Nora. Your words breathe, your cause is nobel and there's fire in you."

"Thank you, for listening and for..." I knew what

she would say. "...Restraining the She-Hulk outburst," I filled in. "That was for the common good actually, so no innocent bystander would get hurt."

"Glad to have you around then," she teased.

"The pleasure is on my side," I smiled at her. The clock ticked by. It was passed 3 p.m. already. "Now that the She-Hulk is tucked away I better sneak away, I have a griffin to catch," I said mysteriously.

"Oh and I have an exam tomorrow," she murmured. "But catching a griffin sounds much more fun, you need to show me how you do that sometime," she chuckled. *If only she knew*, I thought as I bid farewell and exited the restaurant.

4

I walked rapidly to catch the bus. It would take me around an hour to get home. That gave me twelve hours to prepare for Operation Griffin. I felt really dizzy now. The talk with Nora had sucked the energy out of me. My eyelids were stone heavy. I remembered my dream, and that I hadn't slept after that. I would go home, eat something and then hit the sheets for a couple of hours so that I'd be alert for the attack.

I dozed off the moment I sat down in the bus seat. I missed my stop and had to take another bus to get back home. Time was passing by quickly.

I opened the heavy oak door and stepped in. My revolutionary ring tone alerted me and I picked up my phone. It was Haji. He only called when something important had happened.

"Salam," I said, holding my phone tightly to my ear.

"Salam, come online *now*, ImamAli.se has been hacked," he said.

I threw down my jacket on the grey plank floor, grabbed my laptop and ran to my desk.

The first picture in the rotating gallery on the main site, was an image of Imam Ali holding a burning sword, the *Zulfiqar*; given to him by the Prophet, facing demons and Djinn in a battle. Now,

34

it was edited, the demons were still there but Imam Ali was not, only a bloody turban layed on dust with a broken Zulfiqar. All over the site various Wicca, Satanism and New Age symbols were pinned. There was the infamous upside down pentacle, the triquetra, the ankh, the (goat) god, the goddess. They were arranged in a way that Robert Langdon wasn't needed to decipher its meaning. At the top was the all-seeing eye, which I interpreted as "we are watching you". It was as if an army of Djinn had hacked the page and announced war. It wasn't any page, it was a deliberate attack at the only one of the Prophet's companions who was famous for fighting the Djinn, sent to valleys where everyone else returned frightened, he was *always* victorious. I'd later realize that this was my first encounter with the Dark Forces.

I took a screenshot of it and quickly pulled down the page. They hadn't just defaced the landing page, somehow they had executed a SQL injection that had corrupted the database. Or rather, altered the content. At first glance it appeared as if standard "text search and replace" had been used, replacing all occurrences of "Ali" with "Azazel". So, all articles had the word "Imam Azazel" instead of "Imam Ali". That would be simple to fix, I thought, but then I saw that the text replacements were more sophisticated than that. All holy names and places, even words like Ghadir; where the Prophet announced Imam Ali as his successor in the presence of a hundred thousand Muslims, or Zulfiqar, were replaced randomly with different Satanic references and names. Sometimes the randomness seemed intently, such as replacing *Kawthar*, the river in Paradise, with *Maubiqa*; a river of fire in Hell surrounded by huge snakes, just like in the movie "Anaconda". In other places it made no obvious sense, more than them forcing us to restore all articles, by proof reading one by one. Our web hotel had thirty-day database backups so I told Haji to restore the latest database. But, for some reason the scheduled backups were failing each time, meaning we had no backup at all, not even offsite. The page needed to be redone from scratch.

Haji wrote on Slack, *"Emergency meeting tonight at 9 p.m., be there @channel"*. We called ourselves "Nameless Soldiers of the Imam", NSI. We were twelve, six brothers and six sisters. Haji used to call us his *Hawarion*, the twelve disciples of Jesus. NSI's a close-knitted anonymous group working completely covertly. Several of us had their own sub-groups with members and regular meetings, projects, self-building camps and the like. The sub-groups were unaware that their group leaders were members of NSI and reported directly to Haji, and that all the planning was done on a layer above them. The group members participated, discussed and influenced the projects and activities, but all of them were still fulfilling the vision of NSI. They were like crew members on different ships sailing towards the same destination. They choose their seat, uniforms, their boat colors and the like, but ultimately they would arrive at the same end. Sometimes we could collaborate, at important events, and involve all subgroups. Usually that created strong feelings of unification in a shattered *Ummah*. But in reality that was just one of our deliberate plans. All of us had a primary role in the area we operated in, and all of us sat in key positions ranging from mosques, cultural organizations and media.

As the clock ticked by it came to 9 p.m. and Haji turned on his mic. *"Bismillah al-Rahman al-Rahim.* As you might have noticed, our first Imam has been attacked. If you have any *ghoror*, honor, in you, you will not sleep until the site has not only been restored, but enriched with even more content than before. Tell me, what can you do?"

"I can do a powerful spoken word with Hadi", I suggested. Hadi was our multimedia wizard. He was occasionally hired by SVT, the national Swedish Television channel, and also did all the post-editing and effects. He knew the entire Adobe Suite like the back of his hand. Likewise, his gear was only pro material, costing a fortune. So, he lived like an ascetic to afford it with his modest salary. Once he lived on tomato soup for an entire month to buy a new DLSR camera. Now, I didn't like appearing on video but I felt I had no choice. I'd written spoken words for others to perform but they couldn't deliver them with the explosiveness I had loaded the words with. I figured with the correct apparel and some play on light and darkness, and perhaps some post-magic by Hadi, I could perform the poem without being recognized.

"Good," Haji said. "But before doing that, I want you to dig into this attack and see what you can make out of it. Where did it originate from, which vulnerabilities were exploited etc."

"I'm already on it," I said.

Haji himself would re-install the entire site with a new theme, a fresh database and setup some proper security mechanisms to prevent this from happening again.

Fatima, Masuma and Khadija volunteered to proofread, correct and re-upload all articles. Hassan and Zahra would do aggressive marketing to hype the new release. And Jawad would launch a merchandise corner with Imam Ali-related wear; caps, pins, necklaces, wristbands and the like.

"Fatima, Masuma and Khadija, how long time do you need to go through all articles?" Haji said.

"Three days," Masuma answered.

"You have two," Haji said. "I want the site up and running as soon as possible."

"But the spoken word needs longer than that", Hadi said.

"The merchandise production have one week delivery time", Jawad added.

"I know," Haji responded. "The new site will be up within 48 hours, Hassan and Zahra will start dropping teasers of the items you've designed. Ali start writing, Hadi, plan the recording. When the merchandise arrive, Ali should include it in his outfit and we'll release the merchandise corner along with the spoken word, so when viewers have been pumped up by the rhymes, they will start buying immediately."

"Oh and Jawad, one more thing."

"Yes Haji," Jawad said.

"I will design one of the merchandise myself, it will be a burning shield against the satans, among Djinn," Haji said.

And with that, the meeting was over. I picked up the phone and called Haji. "Salam," I said. "What about Operation Griffin? Our time frame is getting smaller for each day."

"I know," Haji said. "I was expecting the Djinn to

do something. They plan, and God plans and God is the best of planners," he quoted the Quran. "But we cannot let Imam Ali's bloody turban lay on the dust, and his site be mocked by their symbols. Work through the night and solve the security issue and commence Operation Griffin tomorrow."

It was almost 2 a.m. My face was immersed in the blueish light shining from the computer screen. A thick fog of darkness surrounded me in the room. The silence was heavy. I could hear my thoughts, feel my heartbeats. The dark clouds were cracked open by the rays of the sun. And that's how I saw him. The Sheikh, the mentor of mentors, the master of contemporary Urefa, Islamic mystics and spiritual wayfarers, Ayatollah Behjat. Even though he had passed away several years ago, no one had filled the void he'd left behind. I'd heard that he continued to provide guidance to his disciples in their dreams, sometimes even performing karamat, miracles, from the other side of Barzakh; the unseen world where the dead souls awaited the Day of Judgement.

"Salam pesar jan, dear son," he said. "You came at last."

"Yes," I said. "I came." I spoke to him for half an hour, asking questions, and for each answer he provided, I felt veils of light being lifted. Even though I couldn't remember the details of the conversation, I felt enlightened.

"Wait here for one of my disciples to arrive, he will guide you further," he said.

I looked at the empty road. Ayatollah Behjat had left me. A tall Seyyed, a black turbaned scholar with direct lineage to Prophet Mohammad, appeared after a while.

"Salam mawla jan, dear master" I said. "I'm hungry."

He bought me ten falafels to eat.

He started walking and I followed him. We arrived at a grand mosque with several floors and huge open spaces. There were trucks and military vehicles. And people, lots of people. A hundred thousand of them. They were waiting for his command. He turned to me, "These people are ready, are you ready?"

I was silent, awestruck.

He handed me a book. "This book is my personal notes on the attacks of Satan, study it, and be prepared," he said.

I woke up. It was almost dawn. The highlighter on the terminal screen on my computer was still ticking. I went to the bathroom to make *wodho* for the night prayers. Just as I was about to start, "I'm a Barbie girl", a disco song from the 90's, started playing in my head. I hated that song, I've never listen to it and I've only heard it play on the radio occasionally. *SobhanAllah*, glory be to God, I thought, the first djinn attack came immediately. I fended of my tone with *istighfar* and *dhikr*.

I started the prayers. At once I got goosebumps, seeing terrifying mental images of demons in front of me, the way they were visualized on horror flicks. At first I got frightened, standing there in the dark room, all alone, surrounded by devils. Then I realized this was the second attack, which I countered with focusing on the words in the prayers and that all power laid in the hands of God; they couldn't hurt me without His permission. I finished the night prayers and did the *fair* prayers. I started feeling a bit stressed out. I needed to investigate the hack attack a bit more before going to school, as later tonight, I had to work on Operation Griffin. I was about to skip my morning Qur'an recitation. Then it struck me, the feeling of baseless stress and worry, the third djinn attack. I opened up the Qur'an and started reading the last page of *Surah Shu'ara*, the 26th chapter, the poets, where I had stopped yesterday:

> And the devils have not brought the revelation down. (210) It is not allowable for them, nor would they be able. (211) Indeed they, from [its] hearing, are removed. (212) [...] Shall I inform you upon whom the devils descend? (221) They descend upon every sinful liar. (222) They pass on what is

heard, and most of them are liars. (223)
[...] Except those who believe and do
righteous deeds and remember Allah often
and defend after they were wronged. And
those who have wronged are going to know
to what [kind of] return they will be
returned. (227)

I felt the words caress my soul like balsam on an
open wound. Total calmness prevailed. The battle
had begun.

5

Love oceans move a divine wave
hungry lovers in the dawn
his oasis is all they crave
scented words ...embracing her
the mirror of your eye
reflects light deep inside illusions
without a guide, lost is your soul
he is the path, You are the goal
pangs of the lover, laying bare
Arise Oh cup bearer,
drink the bowl until you die !

Layla's words touched me, as always. She was a mystery, had she known what I've seen? Or was it just *another* coincidence? I lost thread of my spoken word. Imam Ali's name got replaced with Layla's. Me, being in a spoken word rhyme-mode, I scribbled down a few lines and published them:

From dusk to dawn came a sun of the glorious
one, rays of love turning my stone to bone,
ascending the heart's throne, gnostic lovers
reveal mysteries full blown, sacred lips singing a
divine tone, witnessing divine soldiers alone,
how could she have known?

Yes, it was a bold move, but I was curious, what did she actually know? This public poetic duel was getting more and more personal. It followed me the whole bus trip to school. I don't know exactly when I dozed off by the keyboard last night, but I figured I'd only have had a few hours of sleep. I had one huge lab from 8 a.m. to 5 p.m. and then I'd be free. I passed the day in zombie-mode, yawning every other minute. I set a location based alarm and immediately fell asleep on the bus. I got off at my stop and grabbed a falafel on my way home. It reminded me of my dream, and my dream reminded me of Layla's poem. Had she responded? I devoured the sandwich and sat by my computer. Indeed, she'd written again.

Lilac soul diving to boundless depths
Seduced...... inhale my love
Secrets of her presence... her mystery !
Her aroma steaming from a scented sea
Wine divine !
Embrace these silent breaths
Prisms of life
Whispers intimately.....
Intoxicate this soul this night

Explore me !

I was... bewildered? *Intoxicate this soul this night*, did she mean it like, literally? Tonight? Like now? I didn't really know, nor did I have the time to find out what she meant. I needed to get Operation Griffin going. I sat down by my white desktop. I liked the table white, empty, void of distractions. Beside the laptop I had poured a glass of homemade spearmint lemonade. A secret recipe from Haji, stuffed with Islamic medical wisdom to boost physical and spiritual powers. I called it "Hulk-juice". Focus is more than the intellectual faculty working at its best, it's a window that the soul gazes through; it pierces matter and tries to see the reality of things. Whatever I focus on, there's my soul. I might as well say that focus is the eyes of my soul, and my green drink sharpened my spiritual vision, which was exactly what I needed. *Nora will totally explode into She-Hulk if I offer her this drink*, I grinned before slapping myself and bursting out"Focus!" I downed the glass and set to work.

The white text cursor was blinking on the black Terminal, awaiting my instructions. I listed my encrypted text files and went through the information I'd gathered. Suddenly, I received a red alert from e-jihad. A private message, from Layla.

"What are you seeking?" she wrote.

I'm going to hack the US Air Force, I chuckled. "Top

secret," I typed, "why?"

"You have been summoned," she answered.

"By who? Her Majesty the Queen?"

"The one who gathers the souls."

I started to suspect she actually was intoxicated. But she had my attention, I could give her that.

"What do you mean?" I pressed send.

"At the End of Times the good souls will be gathered within the same movement. There will be many banners, many flags, many symbols, many names - but the movement is *one*," she wrote.

"Ok Wonder Woman, and who are you within this movement?"

"I'm just here to break what needs to be broken, and open what needs to be opened, so you may be granted entrance."

"And how will you do that?"

"Simple. With love."

"You are mere words," I snapped. "How can words crush me open and gush forth love? For all I know you could be a fifty year old perv."

"She smiles."

"Or a gorgeous Amazon with mystical powers, wink wink," she continued.

"Referring to yourself in third person doesn't make you more normal, you know," I wrote and pressed enter. "Nor to write that you wink instead of a wink smiley."

"You are wrong, and right," she wrote.

"Huh?"

"You are right, that I'm not normal, I'm actually pretty weird, according to most standards," she wrote. "But you are wrong, I'm not mere words. What are words? They are an expression of the soul. When we communicate, our souls meet. The Qur'an is also mere words, yet it has a soul, a reality, a spiritual dimension that provides enlightenment to your soul, uplifting you."

"Tell me," she continued, "did you feel anything when I smiled?"

"Yes," I typed reluctantly.

"What did you feel?"

"Warmth." I noticed that I started typing slower, pressing the keys firmly and thoughtfully.

"You know why?" she said. "Because my soul just touched yours."

"Aha. So if you are a sun that makes me what? A flower?"

"She smiles."

"There's a coldness within you," she continued.

"How's that?"

"You've never fallen in love."

I read her words and looked towards the ceiling, sunk in thoughts. As harsh as it sounded, it was true. I've never loved. Well, except a momentary accidental fling in the first grade, I had zero balance in my love account. I was too shy, and later too geeky and after that too religious to make any considerable contact.

"How'd you know?, " I wrote.

"Your poems," she answered.

"What about them?"

"They're good, but they don't move me the way mine moves you. They are mere words."

"He smiles."

"Tee hee."

"Whaaat?! You just transformed from a fifty year old perv to a teenybopper!" I guffawed.

"Yeah, sorry, I have a serious multi personality disorder," she typed.

"I see, Miss Soul Reaper Teenybopper Perv," I teased. "Hope your other personalities are more charming."

"She smiles."

"How can your love be so... real?" I asked.

"I've been through much. I've tasted all kinds of love, and hatred, there is. Ultimately, when I was broken down, in the most desperate state, my rock cracked asunder and forth streamed a pure divine love of unimaginable beauty. I started seeing everything in the light of *that* love. My poetry is mere droplets pouring over from time to time."

"And I've not..."

"...You haven't even tasted love of man, or angels,

let alone God Himself," she responded. "Mullah Sadra says its better for man to love a cat than to love nothing at all."

I pulled up my body and sat down on the chair with crossed legs. I rested by head against my knuckles as I read her words over and over again, thinking, trying to decipher her as if she was some magic formula.

"Do you know Mullah Sadra?" I asked curiously.

"He is one of my favorites," she wrote. "I've studied all of his works."

I hadn't come across a female who's known Mullah Sadra's name, and she claimed to have studied all his works?!

"So you know Persian and Arabic?" I tried in an attempt to figure out her identity. As far as I knew, only one or two of his works were translated to English.

"She smiles."

"You don't need to know Persian and Arabic to study Mullah Sadra, you need to know men who can translate for you," she wrote.

"Oh my," I felt a pang in my heart. "So, Persian men are standing in line to teach you *irfane nazari*, theoretical mysticism?"

"She smiles."

"If you were deserted on an island all alone, kneeling down to God, what would you ask for?"

she continued.

"Perhaps for my faith to be maintained during the difficulties," I typed.

"Why not beg for His love? Why do you matter, you are a mere drop by the ocean. You're prayer rug is that deserted island, imagine begging for His love five times a day!"

I read her words intently. "I haven't thought of it that way, rather that the road is long and difficult and few are the loyal who stand steadfast on the path, I don't want to be a betrayer."

"Do you love Imam Mahdi?" she asked.

"Of course."

"What's the sign of your love?"

"I think of him daily, pray for him, try to actively work in his way by self-building, and in the long run, build up the community in preparation for his arrival," I wrote, feeling proud of my answer.

"What if I told you he has already arrived," she wrote. "What if I told you he is behind you?"

I felt a sudden presence that sent shivers down my spine. I glanced over my shoulder and sensed some new energy surrounding me in the dark room.

"What if I told you he would grant you whatever wish you wanted, what would you tell him?" she wrote.

"I would ask him what I've always prayed for, to

be counted among his friends and those who die for him, in his arms," I typed.

"Why are you so shaped by dogma?" she snapped.

"What do you mean?"

"Well, why do you quote Duaa Ahd?" she wondered. "You have one meeting with the Imam of your time and you cannot think for yourself?"

"So what should I ask for?" I wrote.

"So you want me to think for you? If you'd ever been in love you'd known."

"What would you have asked for?"

"I would have begged him to keep the door of meeting open between us," she typed. "When your love for someone is intense you cannot bear to be without them, even for a moment. Another favorite of mine, Ibn Arabi, opened his poetry work, the *Tarjum al-Ashwaq*, with this very perplexity, the paradox of love: God how can I love You and obey You if You order me to be away from You?!"

"Imam Ali asks this in Duaa Kumail as well, if I'd endure the fire of Hell, how can I endure separation from You?" I typed down my response fast and sent.

"You know your duaas well," she wrote, "Do you know Thawban as well?"

"No." I leaned forth in eagerness to find out who he was.

"Thawban was one of the companions of the Prophet. He wasn't as well-versed in duaa as you. He was just in love. He always attended the Prophet's prayers and was by his side. One day Thawban wasn't there and the Prophet got worried. After inquiring about him, the Prophet was told that Thawban was at home, sick. The Prophet went visiting him and found Thawban in a miserable state; yellow skin, pale face, sweaty, feverish. 'What has happened to you?' the Prophet asked."

I impatiently waited for her to tell me more.

She continued, "Yesterday the most frightening thought occurred to me. I realized that I'm nothing compared to your rank, I will not be able to visit you and enjoy your nearness in the next life as much as I do here. And that caused me such great grief that I'm now in this state,' Thawban said. Then the following verse from the Holy Qur'an was revealed to the Prophet."

My eyes ran through her words as she was pasting the verse.

> And whoever obeys Allah and the
> Messenger - those will be with the ones
> upon whom Allah has bestowed favor of the
> prophets, the steadfast affirmers of truth, the
> martyrs and the righteous. And excellent are

those as companions. (4:69)

"Look at this love of Thawban! Nobody taught him that! He didn't read it in a book or hear it from some sage! It originated from his heart, because he was *in* love!"

I was dumbfounded.

"I must go," I wrote.

"Why?" she asked.

"I feel sad."

"Then cry."

And I did, I cried. I rolled out my prayer rug in front of my open window and prostrated. Like a broken tree, falling into a river, my body trembled whilst my tears poured down. I felt like a snail, imagining my hollow shell to be a precious treasure. And in the blink of an eye, a boot cracks it asunder, dawning the obvious truth of emptiness all along.

> *I long to see your full moon*
> *Listen to my sorrowful tune*
> *O Lord, at your door I kneel*
> *Please, your homeless dog heal*

I looked up and my tears were enshrouded in the moon shine, like the glittering stars in the midnight sky. I recalled the words from Duaa 'Ahd, *"Show me the praiseworthy moon"*, then I thought of Layla's words, *Don't be a parrot, repeating what you have been taught, be an artist of the heart*, I told myself. I grabbed a pen and poured down the lines to depict my state:

> *A lonely midnight breeze*
> *sweep through the moon shine's soul*
> *a dancer in the dark it seize*
> *whirling into the depths*
> *his heart in agony freeze*
> *unspoken words whisper*
> *a beautiful face he sees*
> *Kissing love's sweetness*
> *forcing his spirit on knees*
> *crystal tears cover longing*
> *ascending into passionate degrees*

I laid down on the prayer rug, and rolled over to the side, exhausted. My eyelids swallowed the moon as I drifted away into a silent sleep.

I could see a road ahead of me. On it stood a beautiful white horse, and beside it, a handsome man. He was stroking the horse on its back. He wore a green turban and a black cloak above his white robe. He had a dark beard and deep mysterious eyes, like the endless starlit sky. I approached him. "Salam," I greeted.

He looked up at me. "Wa alaykoma salam."

"Who are you?" I asked.

"Jafar Sadiq," he said.

Then he mounted the horse and rode into the sky.

6

I woke up with a heavy head, just before the dawn prayer, again. God, I thought, I completely forgot about Operation Griffin last night. Then I thought of him, Imam Jafar Sadiq, the founder of the Shi'ite school of Islamic jurisprudence and the teacher of all the founders of the four Sunni schools. The thought made me shiver. I kept thinking of my dream the whole way to school. What did the white horse symbolize?

As I entered the school yard, my reflections shattered. Nora was surrounded by the Haram Police. She was wearing really tight clothes, her ankles clearly visible, her sleeves pulled up to display all her bracelets, and the scarf wrapped in a way that exposed her black feather earrings. I could see how they eyed her from tip to toe. The rage was pounding inside of me. With no spark of decency, they didn't let her pass, yelling profanities, telling her to take off her veil and not embarrass all sisters with proper hijab. Then I lost it. I ran, out of instinct, and found myself pushing away one of them, the guy slided several meter away. I felt like the Hulk, was this some Hulk juice effect? Another one of them jumped forth and threw a punch at me. Heart beating like crazy, I dodged to the left, hit him hard in the stomach with the right fist and kicked him away in the chest. He fell on the floor panting, not grasping what had hit him. I turned and saw Farooq, their alpha, hurrying towards me, but I was to late to stop his grip on me. He held me in tightly, while another one approached me from the front. Eyes blackened with fury, I lifted both legs and kicked him hard so that I flew backwards with Farooq, landing atop him. I turned around and was about to finish him off when the sight of Imam Jafar Sadiq flashed and I stopped my fist mid air. I saw Nora in chock, crying. I let myself cool, then stood up and led her away.

"Let's get out of here," I told her.

"I want to go home," she said through her tears.

As we started walking I heard Farooq's rapid breaths approaching from behind. I pushed Nora to the right, moved and dodged his punch and turned around in one movement and threw my right fist. *Boom*, it hit Farooq's cheek with a perfect impact throwing him to the ground. He blacked out.

"Let's go," I said to Nora, feeling the ache in my fist.

Nora just lived a few blocks away in a small student apartment. Our walk was cold and windy. We were silent, letting the chock subside. *What would have happened if Imam Sadiq didn't appear? I* thought for myself. It was his clement face that had stopped my volcano from erupting. The thoughts faded away as we went inside and I got hit by a warm and sweet fragrance. Nora's apartment was really cozy. Lots of scented candles, walls decorated with soft materials, photos of various women with feathers, a dark purple armchair with a wool sheet on it. She sat down on her bed, shivering. I took the wool sheet and put it on her shoulders and pulled the armchair, seating myself in front of her.

"How are you?" I asked.

She was silent.

"I know that you're in pain, but know that one day your pain will be your cure," I tried. "To love is human, to feel pain is human, but to still love whilst in suffering, that's divine. Your wound is the place where the light enters."

She kept silent. And I kept going.

"They can try to bury you, but you are like a seed, from your burial will gush forth a strong, fruitful tree that will be the refuge of the sunburnt and hungry."

No sound.

"Just know that God sees, the mere knowledge that He sees your struggle is uplifting," I continued.

"Sometimes, I think about just taking it off." She

sobbed.

"What?"

"The hijab. I don't fit into its framework, its message, its domain."

"Why not?"

"Just look at me. I like to be expressive. To make a statement. The hijab stands for modesty, is it modest to scream your emotions?"

"Make a statement," I moved forth, resting the elbows on my knees, looking straight at her, "but don't limit it to your body. Hijab is more than a dress, it's a state of the mind. Like a spiritual state, like a Karate costume you dress your soul with. Both in defense against oppression, and as an attack to it."

"But I don't want to wear a baggy black abaya," she rebuked. "That's so not me!"

"Then don't," I comforted. "There is a voice that you cannot hear, except when in silence, find it inside you, listen to it, and let it dictate the way you dress. Besides, super tight clothes aren't really healthy for you."

"Why not," she murmured.

"First of all, it's Sweden so its freezing cold."

And she smiled at that.

"Secondly, your skin needs to breath, when you take on tight polyester leggings, it's like covering your head with a tiny plastic bag." I grimaced.

She laughed. I smiled back.

"Anyhow, I think you should do whatever suits you, reflects your degree of passion and faith, and build on that, not because someone else, especially males, tell you. Stay true to yourself and your ideals," I reassured.

She smiled. "I'll be right back," I said.

I went to the kitchen and made some cinnamon tea.

"Drink this," I said, handing her the cup.

She looked at me with her big green eyes. "Did you rummage around my apartment?" she teased.

"I was actually looking for the bathroom," I said.

"Inside the kitchen?"

"Of course, where else would they put it?"

We both laughed.

She drank her tea. "I want to lay down," she whispered.

"Do it."

I pulled the curtains and she fell asleep. I observed her, her little neat nose, her round soft chins, her long dark eyelashes, her eyebrows - contrasting her bright skin, her ample, dark red lips, the small chocolate brown mole above them. I knew I had to leave before she'd become irresistible. As if she had read my mind, she suddenly opened her eyes and saw me staring at her. "Please, don't go," she whispered. "You help me calm down."

I hesitated, but finally nodded. "Thank you," she said, then closed her eyes and fell asleep.

I pulled out my laptop and sat down on the floor. Haji had written on Slack, "Everything is done. ImamAli.se is up and running. We will release it tonight after Duaa Kumail (the famous prayer of Imam Ali, highly recommended to read on Thursday nights. He used to read it himself while being in *sujood*, prostrated on the ground, crying all the time)."

All articles were up and so was the new content and videos. Haji posted a photo of the merchandise he had designed himself. It was a beautiful brown leather *Ayn Ali* bracelet with a copper amulet. Ayn Ali is a powerful supplication against evil, especially protective against djinn and demons. "You will receive one when we meet," he promised.

I put down my laptop. Nora's curtains were keeping the light out, making me sleepy. My body hurt from the fight and the room was too cozy to resist laying down. I put some ice in a bag for my sore fist, fetched another blanket and pillow and laid down on the thick furry carpet. *Just for a moment*, I thought. I hadn't slept much lately. And so, I drifted away.

A couple of hours later I started gaining consciousness, feeling very warm. I opened my eyes and realized why. Behind me laid Nora, holding me close. I felt her moist breaths in my neck. Her soft toes were pressed around my ankles. I panicked, not knowing what to do. I tried to move away but she held me tight. The She-Hulk talk was no joke. She murmured in her sleepy voice how she would never let go of me.

I started making a *dhikr*, but my body wouldn't cooperate. I was infused with a weak scent of jasmine, coming from her body. I felt like a prisoner, but in a good one. I laid still and closed my eyes. The face of Imam Jafar Sadiq appeared again. He had mounted the white horse and was about to ride into the sky, when he reached out his hand to me. I touched it and felt a tremendous tremble. It broke me free from the shackles of lust. I opened my eyes, gathered all strength I had and rose up. "Don't leave me," she said. "I'll feel worthless."

"I'm not leaving you," I told her, "I'm lifting you." Then I turned away and left, closing the door behind me.

I ran to the bus and then ran all the way from the bus home. I stepped in, closed the door behind me and fell down on my knees, crying and shaking. Short-lived, gigantic, waves of rage and lust had broken me so thoroughly, leaving me sobbing behind a door. I'd never even kissed a girl and have always had a romantic notion of kissing my *wife* for the first time. That dream was almost shattered now, if it wasn't for Imam Jafar Sadiq. I was indebted to him and I had to repay it, showing my gratitude, by commercing Operation Griffin, *now*.

I fired up the computer and launched the Terminal again. E-jihad alerted me of some high priority news. I read that the police was going through Stakkato's files and had found thousands of passwords for very sensitive companies and institutions. Time's running out. SÄPO, the Swedish security services, could discover the login to the US Air Force anytime now, and inform their American counterparts of the breach.

I didn't get any further than that when my inbox pinged.

"Salam," Layla wrote.

"Salam," I responded.

"He raped me."

Her words felt like a stab to my heart.

"Who raped you?!"

"My husband."

"Your husband? Are you married?" I swallowed a stone.

"We're getting divorced."

"What happened?" I switched position and started moving my leg up and down anxiously.

"I'd just put Sara, my daughter, to sleep and went

to the kitchen to prepare a meal. My husband came in and got really close. I pushed him away and reminded him that we were getting divorced. He wouldn't listen. He said he wouldn't let anyone have me and that I was his. He yelled at me, I tried to defend myself but he gripped my hands really hard, turned me around and pressed me down over the countertop, then he pulled down my trousers and raped me." Reading her words caused such an agony. I was gasping for air, yet sealed to the screen to find out more.

"I felt like a twig cracked from the inside out. I begged him to stop, but he just kept going. I pressed my hand to my mouth so that Sara wouldn't hear my sobs and witness this. He got encouraged by my lack of sound, his panting increased and he felt like a hungry wolf chasing its prey. Finally, when he was done he just left me there, leaking and bruised, and went out. I feel disgusted with myself. I've showered and scrubbed myself over and over again but his smell won't go away. Oh, I don't know Ali, I'm crying."

Tears rolled down my check. I was baffled and my heart ached for her. I typed, "I feel so sad for you. It hurts me to hear this. Can't you leave the house?"

"Where'd I go? I don't know anyone."

"Come to Stockholm. I'll arrange everything.

Pack your bags, I'll give you a call within the hour, what's the closest airport?"

"Stansted," she replied.

I found a RyanAir flight departure to Stockholm, for a small price that even my monthly student budget could pay, without using any of my reserves. I called up Haji and briefed him of the situation, not mentioning any personal details, just that a sister was in trouble and needed somewhere to stay with her daughter for sometime. He called me back thirty minutes later, Masuma had offered her home. She was a teacher in her late twenties. She was still unmarried but had moved out to her own neat little apartment in one of the suburbs in Stockholm. She was a very kind soul, enlightened, putting all her spare time into reading, drinking tea and growing plants in her glass balcony.

I called Layla.

"Yes?", she answered.

"I've arranged for everything, there's a sister in Stockholm that has offered her home for you, and I've looked at tickets on RyanAir, there is a flight in a couple of hours, so I figured you just take a cab to the airport and I'll buy the ticket for you." Gosh, I babbled with a weird voice. I probably sounded like a frog.

"Is this Ali?" Her voice was softly hoarse. I could sense the anticipation in her breaths.

"Oh yes, sorry I forgot to introduce myself, yes I'm Ali, your MuslimChat rival poet, he he he." I bit my underlip and made a fun grimace out of awkwardness, still sounding like a sweaty frog.

"It's nice to hear your voice," she said. And breathed out.

7

When the red alarm lamp started flashing at the IT department of Naval Air Station Patuxent River the employees got bewildered. The alarm had never gone off before. It took a while until they oriented themselves and understood what was going on.

"Sir, we got a situation."

"Yes?"

"Someone is inside our system, and I don't mean scratching on the firewall, in, like really in."

"What?! How is that possible?!"

"I don't know, come and take a look."

Dr. Mike Owens was the best in his class. He graduated with highest regards from MIT in Computer Science and was soon after recruited by the military to its cyber warfare division. Later on, he joined the American Air Force and now had the role as head of security, with undiminished reputation. At least, until now.

He fired up a Terminal and executed some commands rapidly, now and then rubbing his finger tips with his thumbs.

"It can't be... unless... but that's impossible...!" he said to himself. "Miss Johnsson, call the Director, immediately."

"Yes, sir!"

Dr. Owens grabbed the phone.

"Good day sir, this is Owens, we have an intruder inside our firewall," he said with a calm but serious tone.

"How?" the director asked.

"It seems he has a valid login since I cannot see any traces of any kinds of attacks or intrusion attempts," Owens replied.

"Can you trace him?" the director snapped.

"Already did that. The hacker is coming from Technion University," Owens said.

"Israel?! Why would our allies do that? That makes no sense."

"No, unless the hacker has access to some computer at the university and uses it as a tunnel to our servers," Owens played with a pen on the desk in a reflective state.

"But how can he have a valid authentication," the director said.

"I don't know, we don't have any known security breaches as far as I know, unless, of course, the data breach was several years ago but wasn't used until now."

"Clever," the director said. "Shut down the account and see if you can trace the origins of the attack. This smells like the involvement of some government, possibly China."

"Indeed, thank you sir," Owens said and hung up.

Owens put on his headphones and went into *the zone*. His fingers danced across the keyboard. He was Bach, executing line after line of digital music. Fifteen minutes later he threw up a complex scheme, plotted with boxes and arrows, unto the main screen.

"Can someone tell me what this is?" he asked his staff.

A minute of silence, then someone said, "It seems like the routing of the hacker."

"Exactly," Owens said. "It shows where the hacker entered, his route across our filesystem, and where he exited."

They all watched the printouts of all the directories and files and systems that the hacker had accessed in absolute silence. Then came the shriek. Owens dropped his coffee mug.

"Miss Johsson, get me the director, now."

"Yes, sir!"

Owens picked up the phone. "Hello sir, this is Owens, again."

"Yes?"

"We now know what the hacker was after," Owens said.

"Tell me," the director said.

"He accessed the Patuxent River Naval Air Systems command," Owens stopped.

"And?", the director said impatiently.

"It seems he copied the schematics and blueprints for the F-18," Owens said nervously.

"Jesus. Christ," the director said, "how could he have done that?!"

"He had root access," Owens said.

"What?! How did he get that?" the director screamed.

"I don't know sir."

After a moment of silence the director exclaimed, "I need to call the President"

"I think that would be a good idea sir," Owens said as the director hung up.

Meanwhile in Malmö

"Allahu Akbar, Allahu Akbar! Ash-hado an la illaha ill Allah! Ash-hado an la illaha ill Allah!"

I made the *Azan*, the call to prayers, with full tranquility. I felt like a flute, playing the divine melody. I performed *fajr*, the dawn prayer, with excellent focus. Then I recited the Holy Quran with a voice that moved me to tears. I put my head on a pillow and dozed off.

I rose up, not my body, but my soul. I turned, standing at the feet of my body, I watched myself, my physical self, laying there with closed eyes, sleeping with a small smile, as I, my soul, ascended upwards, through heavens, through layers, until I reached above the clouds, a voice echoed, "Open your eyes, if you wish to see the eternal light!" I opened them and saw an immensely bright light shine everywhere and in all directions.

I checked my watch, it was morning already. I grabbed the phone and wrote on Slack, "In one of his poems the great Persian poet and mystic Hafez narrates the following story, attractively, using beautiful metaphors:

'An old seer and sage told me the following story, which I shall never forget: One day a pious man was going somewhere. On his way he saw a drunkard sitting, who said, 'Devotee, if you have some bait to offer, lay down your trap here.'

'I have a trap but I want to catch a *griffin*,' the devotee said.

'You can catch it only if you know where it is to be found. But its nest is not known', the drunkard said.

'That's right, but to be disappointed is a worse calamity,' said the devotee."

Then I wrote, "Obviously, it's not possible to catch the griffin when its nest is not known. But Allah can bestow His favor and help His lover to catch the griffin, *alhamdulillah*."

Within seconds Haji reacted to the post with an

"Allahu Akbar" emoji and then called to a meeting later that day. He wrote to me privately, "You should get some rest Ali," caring as always.

"I will Haji, thanks," I responded and put aside the phone. The memories from last night flashed by as I drifted into sleep, smiling.

Owens pounded his keyboard, pausing only to scratch his stubble or rub his fingertips whilst he was thinking. Profanities was not his thing, but now he was heard cursing occasionally. After several hours of deep diving and plotting the cyberattack he had ended up in Linköping University, where he couldn't get any further without assistance from the local IT guys. He called up the director again, "Good day sir," he said. "I think I know the origin of the hacker now."

"Yes?"

"Well, it seems he has travelled to several university computers around the globe, even from within the US, and then he knocked on our door. To have used the Israeli computer as his last exit node must have been some sort of political satire from his part. Anyhow, it seems he originates from Sweden, or at least that's where his traces end. I can't see any further than that."

"I will call the Swedish authorities, pack your bag, you're taking the next flight to Sweden."

"Yes, sir!"

"*Bismillah Rahman Rahim*, brothers and sisters, please send a *salawat*, peace and blessings upon Prophet Mohammad and his family," Haji said, starting the meeting. "By the grace of Allah, last night we successfully executed an operation that will bring a drastic change upon the military world as we know it. This will soon be out in the news so I want you to hear it from me first. Our brother Ali has extracted blueprints from the American Air Force. Using them, anyone with the money and resources can manufacture their own fire jets."

All the members of NSI chanted the *takbir*, Allahu Akbar, with hopeful voices. I, however, was silent.

"Let me enlighten you of how unprecedented this is," Haji continued. "Very few nations have the ability to design, develop and manufacture their own modern fighter jets. The only nations who can do so are the US, Russia, France, China, India, South Korea and of course Sweden, with its Gripen. Those who have the fighter jets, also rule the air space in multiple ways. We will change that."

"What is the plan now?" Hadi asked, sounding eager.

"I will take the Saturday flight to Iran and hand

over the blueprints to the commander of the Islamic Forces," Haji explained. "As you might understand that will significantly alter the military situation in the Middle East."

"When Iran landed the US drone it didn't take long for them to reproduce their own drones, and also hand over the technology to their allies in Lebanon. Then came news reports of drones gathering surveillance in Israel," Masuma said.

"If Iran has its own state of the art Air Force production rather than a couple of rusty left overs from the Shah, USA and its allies won't stand a chance in Syria, Lebanon, Palestine or the rest of the region!" Hassan filled in zealously.

"That's the idea," Haji said. "Beware though, this is a huge move, which means it's not gone unnoticed, neither by the governments nor by Iblis and his army. They will attack us one way or the other, so be vigilant." And as such, Haji concluded the meeting.

Owens was jet-lagged when he stepped into Linköping University's IT department. He went straight into the meeting with Peter Larsson, head of security at the university, Johan Falkenberg, from SÄPO and a few other staff members. Owens summarized the series of events and concluded the President was informed and considered this issue a top priority matter. After Falkenberg's thorough presentation, everything became clear for Owens. Falkenberg mentioned the Stakkato attack and all the logins to various university computers and super computers around the globe that they had digested, including root access to Patuxent River Naval Air Systems.

"Why didn't you brief us earlier?!" Owens yelled out.

"This intel was undisclosed just now," Falkenberg countered. "The hard drives we confiscated contained thousands and thousands of accounts, so it took a while to go through."

"Well that means the hacker probably isn't someone at the Linköping University," Owens looked at Larsson. "Can we dig further and see where the connection originates from?"

"Probably," Larsson said.

"My job here is to trace the hacker," Owens said.

"If you trace him, we'll catch him," Falkenberg reassured. "You have all the resources that you need."

Owens straightened the sleeves of his shirt. "Thank you. The President probably expects the criminals to be handed over to US authority."

"We'll see about that," Falkenberg said. "But considering Sweden's track record of extraditing criminals that probably won't be a problem."

The meeting was concluded. Owens and Larsson went into Larsson's office to start working right away.

8

"Laqis!"

"Yes, master."

"Are you aware of what the NSI is up to?"

"Yes, master. We have the situation under control."

"How?"

"In their last meeting their leader Mohsen Hajizadeh announced his plans, what to do with the blue prints."

"Those prints cannot reach the Iranians, do you hear me Laqis?!"

"Yes, master. They will not. We are working on one of the younger NSI members. We will convert him at the right moment and use him to confiscate the blueprints and abolish their plan."

"What's his weakness?"

"He's their media guy, a simple student with great ambitions and an exaggerated love for tech gear. I've already pulled one of my Hollywood directors. We will offer him some artistic appreciation to massage his vanity, and then offer him a job he cannot refuse, as it'll give him an unlimited tech arsenal, an unlimited budget, a fat salary and ultimately acknowledgement by recognized critics."

"Sounds good, what else do you have in store?"

"Their hacker, Ali, we cannot convert him to our cause. We can however slow him down and distract him."

"What did you have in mind?"

"Love of a, or in this case, two women. He is a naive virgin with a strong empathic side. We are using that to snare him in, entangle him and distract him. We also have one of our Andalusian men with a great taste for spirituality and poetry, who might be introduced later. The perfect setup for a broken heart."

"Very good Laqis, patient as always, taking one step at a time, waiting for the perfect moment to deliver the death stroke. Can you whisper some ideas to Owens to speed up his process of finding Ali?"

"Unfortunately, not. Ali used a password manager, so we never saw him typing any of the actual passwords, and he kept erasing all logs and traces. We simply don't know what he's done and how he's done it."

"What about Hajizadeh, do we have anything on him?"

Laqis grinned.

"I was waiting for you to bring it up master. Actually, we do."

"Tell me more."

"We are aiming at capturing the blueprints

together with Hajizadeh. If we succeed with that, then he will be captured and tucked away silently under the new counter-terrorism police, we recently established within SÄPO."

"Jail?"

"No, worse. He will end up being drugged for the rest of his life in a mental hospital."

"And if you don't succeed in capturing him with the blueprints?"

"Then our mole within the Islamic Forces will setup an even worse outcome."

"Go on."

"When Hajizadeh meets with his contact at the Islamic Forces in Iran, we will arrange a car crash for his contact's wife. Nothing lethal, just enough to make him go to the hospital and send his assistant instead, our mole. The meeting will be documented and photographed covertly. A week later. our mole will travel to Israel and hand over the blueprints. Israel will announce that it has come over the blueprints. At the same time, the news will hit the Iranian public that a Mossad agent has been working within the Islamic Forces. Shortly thereafter, we will leak the photos of the meeting between Hajizadeh and our mole, the Mossad agent, and the media will take care of the rest."

"He'll be treated as a traitor, a hypocrite, tortured and hanged."

"Yes, master," Laqis said.
An evil laughter echoed in the dark chamber.

9

Short after midnight Owens and Larsson had localized the origins of the attack. The tracks ended at Lund's Technical University. They crashed on the sofas. And just at 6 a.m., Falkenberg stormed in with fresh brewed coffee. "Let's go," he said. They packed their laptops, jumped into Falkenberg's civil police car, a turbo loaded Volvo V60, turned on the silent blue light and slammed the pedal. It was a four and half hour long drive to Lund, but with Falkenberg's pace they covered the distance in two hours, just in time for the reception to open and the personnel to start their workday.

I woke up with a rapid heartbeat. *SobhanAllah, what a dream*, I thought. I called Haji immediately. It was still early but no one woke up before Haji. He was the last to sleep at night and the first to wake, before dawn. I don't think he gets more than four hours of sleep at night, yet his energy level's incredible.

"Haji, I had a troubling dream," I told him.

"Go on," he said with a calm voice.

"I dreamt of the NSI. We were going on a journey. I recited a heartily poem saying that we, ourselves, *were* the journey. We then mounted air balloons and started ascending towards the skies, towards the light. But a situation arouse and for some reason Hadi jumped overboard, towards a certain death. You and I immediately jumped after him, then I reached for his parachute and pulled it. All three of us landed calmly on the ground. We looked up and there was Kabah, with all its glorious might, shining in front of us. But Hadi had his back towards it and watched out towards the glimmers of the city lights below us. Then I woke up."

"I see," Haji said. "Well, our life is a journey, for each moment that passes we take one step, so we need to be cautious not to walk astray, and vigilant to make the most out of it, so we blossom in the end, rather than wither."

I pondered on what he said. Sometimes it felt as if Haji spoke in riddles with deeper meanings that unravelled themselves as time passed by.

"What should I do with Hadi?" I asked.

"He is coming to Stockholm today, give him the USB drive," Haji said.

"Are you sure?"

"Yes, I've already spoken with him, he is prepared and aware of the severity of the mission."

"Ok, should I come with him then?"

"No you cannot leave the area, soon all hell will break loose and I need you to be near your office in case something happens. Also, I don't want you to draw any attention to yourself," Haji cautioned.

"I understand. Should I tell Hadi about my dream?"

"Write it on Slack. Let all members know. I will ask them to write what they think it means afterwards," Haji ended the call.

Falkenberg showed his SÄPO badge and headed into the security room together with Owens and Larsson. Mats Lindström, the head of IT for LTH, and some developers were also present. With some teamwork they could pinpoint the exact room and computer the attack originated from. According to the logs the intrusions started on Tuesday night, around 10 p.m. The university was locked after 9 p.m., but students could access the facilities using keycards. The keycards however weren't personal. Also the hacker could have sticked around after closing hours. But one thing was pretty sure, it was probably a student.

"Can you lookup from which computer the attack was made?" Owens said.

"Computer six in the computer lab, on the second floor," Lindström said.

"Do we have any surveillance footage from the lab?" Owens asked.

Lindström shook his head. "I'm afraid not. We don't have many surveillance cameras, apart from the main entrances."

Owens facepalmed himself. "Right, I forgot we're in Sweden. Then show me the user logs of the computer for the day."

Lindström made a few quick moves on the keyboard and squinted, "Hmm, interesting. It seems that one student used the computer from 4 p.m. until late night"

"Bingo!" Owens exclaimed.

To remind them of his presence Falkenberg raised his voice. "Print me his photo and schedule, I'll take it from here."

"Yes, sir!"

I met Hadi on my way to school.

"Salam brother, how are you?" I said.

"Fine *alhamdulillah*, what about you?" Hadi said.

"A bit weary but I'm ok. I have an USB drive for you to deliver to Haji," I said.

"Yeah, I heard. I'll take it, thanks." And then he left.

There was something strange going on. Hadi was usually jocose, always having a broad smile on his lips. He was a bit plump and radiated a kind warmness. Our own huggable bearded bear, we called him. But even though I held him in my arms when I bid him farewell, there was a miles distance between our hearts. I watched him walk down the road and couldn't help but feel pity for him.

Hasbunallah wa n'emal wakil - God is sufficient and the best advocate, I thought.

When I arrived at the schoolyard, the Taliban Squad surrounded me. Farooq stepped forth. His face was full of rancor. I held my stance, not moving, but observing that they'd both caged me in and obstructed the view from bypassers. Farooq took out a jack knife from his pocket. The sun glare indicated the knife was well grounded and sharp. I held my breath, not afraid, but rather estimating the outcome of this confrontation. I discreetly buckled up my belt and held the anchor in my hand. I had only trained one session in using the belt as a weapon with my *Sifu*, but I had nothing else within reach so it had to do. Our eyes were fixed on each other. The battle started there, the psychological battle, the spiritual fight, the war of the souls. We both breathed silently, not moving. My heart beat hard, waiting for the signal to burst blood into the body. For him: to move his knife towards my stomach. For me: to block the stab attempt with my left hand as I pull out my belt with the right hand and slide behind him to entangle and choke him. The wind blew hard in our faces. The situation was just about to explode when a scream distracted us both. It was Nora from across the schoolyard who saw what's been going down. Then it all happened so fast. One police car and one civil car with blue lights pulled up. A person, looking like an agent with his dark costume, stepped out of the civil car followed by two police officers. He walked towards us. Farooq handed over the knife to his friend behind him.

The agent stood in front of me and Farooq, eying us with a stern look.

"Arrest him," Falkenberg ordered.

I tried to slow down my breathing but my heart was in a frenzy.

The police men took out their handcuffs.

"Farooq Abdul-Aziz, you are under arrest for threat towards national security and unauthorized access to classified systems," Falkenberg said sternly and continued to read Farooq's rights as the men handcuffed him. I was still watching as they escorted Farooq to the police car when Nora jumped into my arms taking me by surprise. I felt her warm scent even though two thick jackets separated our bodies.

"Are you ok?" she asked me.

"Yeah, a bit shaken, but ok," I murmured.

"Come, let's go for a cup of coffee," she said as she dragged me along. I couldn't say no.

She wiped the Americano crema off her lips. I realized they were pinker than the last time we'd seen each other. I was whisking my brown sugary honey filled latte macchiato.

"I like my coffee sweet," I said.

She chuckled. "Yeah, I can see that."

"I like how the black coffee drops mingle with the white foam. How, the way black and white intertwine and makes everything brown. Yet, amid all chaos, the white still prevails at the top," I continued, looking seriously at her.

"So what just happened?" she said, meeting my serious look.

"Do you really want to know?"

She leaned her chin on her crossed hands. "Yes, of course Ali. Please tell me."

I noticed how long eye lashes she had, the dark contours enhanced with mascara.

"After I left you the other day, after the Taliban Squad had assaulted you, I went back home. I returned later that afternoon for some schoolwork. When I entered the computer lab on the second floor, Farooq and one of his followers were sitting there." I paused to take a sip from my latte. "Of course, the fire between us hadn't settled. There were a few heated exchanges before Farooq tried to punch me. I dodged and kicked him so he flew back, but his friend pushed me from behind so I lost balance and fell on the ground."

As I was speaking Nora was sitting completely still, apart from her eyelashes occassionally falling and rising as she blinked.

"Right then, a teacher and some other students came in. Since both of them were standing while I was laying down, the teacher concluded that they had jumped me so he threw them out of the lab. When Farooq exited the room, he whispered in my ear that it wasn't over. What happened today was a realization of that threat."

What I didn't tell Nora was that during all the turmoil, Farooq had forgotten to log out of his computer. I saw it as a golden opportunity and sat down by his desk. From there I started putting Operation Griffin in action, masked behind Farooq's identity.

"Where did you learn to fight like that?" Nora said. I could sense the subtle amazement in her tone.

"Growing up as a skinny immigrant kid with no siblings, was kind of tough," I said. "And my childhood heroes were Bruce Lee and Jackie Chan. So when my *Sifu* opened up a Kung Fu school in Lund, I jumped onboard and trained like crazy. To be honest, I didn't have many other interests. Tooth bracelets, afro hair, skinny body and not being allowed to leave the house after dark, is a good cocktail to kill anyone's self esteem."

"So you went training for all the party fights that you wouldn't participate in," she teased. There was her little chuckle again.

"Yep, Kung Fu and religion, that was my thing. Training my body at day and my mind at night. But it helped me build my identity, who I am, and along came the confidence and the resolute willpower," I stretched my back and sat upright. "But there's a lot of spirit in you as well, where'd you get that from?"

"An abusive father and a super feminist mother," she retorted.

"Oh my, tell me more!"

"My father is Moroccan. He has religious roots, but found alcohol when he came to Sweden. I guess that was his therapy for all the crap he went through back home. He was always kind to me but his roots surfaced when he drank," she sighed.

"Did he surpress his background?", I asked.

"I guess so. He became all religiously romantic after a couple of drinks. He had a soft spot for the veil and Islamic tradition, which he used to tell me about when drunk. Often it ended in tears because he couldn't pray in that state, so he'd start reciting spiritual poetry and weep. But my mother hated it."

"Why?"

Nora leaned back on the chair and looked out the window, feeling suddenly distant. "She grew up during the secular anti-religious rhetorics of

Atatürk. She thought Islam was oppressive towards women, especially the hijab. So naturally they would get into nasty fights. He brainwashed his daughter to wear hijab, that is how she saw it anyways."

Nora didn't look at me as she spoke. I could feel the hurt suppressed in her voice.

"She'd cross the line and say demeaning words against religion and my father would snap. He felt that she disrespected his heritage, and with alcohol, all barriers to his self-restraint were removed. He'd hit and abuse her."

"With your past, I guess you're not in good terms with your mother now, considering you have the hijab?" I said.

"No. She feels betrayed, hates the way I dress and she thinks that I've taken sides with dad," she sobbed. "That's why I moved to my own apartment when I was eighteen."

"What happened to your dad," I asked.

"He moved back to Marocco around the same time."

We looked at each other. There was a moment of silence. When a soul undresses its veils and comes bare to the field, vulnerabilities exposed, it's beautiful. Few reach this stage of trust, even after years of friendship or marriage.

There is a field inside my soul, I'll meet you there, I

thought.

"You should visit your father sometime," I said. "Discover your origins."

"Yeah, I know, but..."

"Your mother. I know," I said.

She looked down. I could see her overwhelmed with emotions. I took out my phone and started playing Sami Yusuf's "Guide me home".

> THIRSTY AS A DESERT'S PAIN
> I MISS YOUR TOUCH LIKE POURING RAIN
> WHEN CLOUDS COME IN THEY CRY ALL NIGHT
> AND GIVE ME TEARS TO FILL MY EYES
> THE FOOTPRINTS THAT YOU LEFT HAVE STAYED
> ABOVE THE SAND BENEATH THE WAVES
> LONG AFTER TIME HAS LET THEM GO
> I'LL WAIT FOR TIDES TO GUIDE YOU HOME

Drops of tears fell on the brown coffee table.

"The love a mother has for her child is ungraspable," I consoled. "Until you have one of your own. Give her some time. She's just afraid that you might end up oppressing yourself, not standing on your own feet. Or worse, that you become one of the extremists she fought against. "

"I don't know," she mumbled.

"If she only knew what brave soul you are, and how you stand against the same mindset she resents."

She looked down at the table. "I'm not brave, just rowdy."

"So you are *not* the She-Hulk?" I teased.

A small smile broke her cloudy grief.

"My exam starts in 15," she said.

"Let's go."

10

The rest of the day passed by with little drama. Haji posted a photo in Slack with him and Hadi having Indian food, and another one of two gigantic mango lassi drinks. I was tired. It was as if my body had been drained of me, my soul, and laid like a cloth piece on my bed. It'd been an intensive week. As I was about to sleep, my phone vibrated. It was Layla, I'd totally forgotten about her.

"Salam," I answered.

"Salam," she said. There was that soft hoarse voice again. The blood started pumping and I could sense how the heat turned my ears red.

"How are you? How's everything going?" I said.

"It's good, thank you. Masuma is an angel and Sara is fond of her and wants to sit on her lap all the time."

"That makes me happy," I smiled to myself. "How are things at home?"

"That's one of the reasons I called." She sounded worried. "Today the police came to my apartment and arrested my husband."

"Did you press charges?" I said.

"No, but apparently he had tried to hit on another younger girl and it had all escalated very badly, so they arrested him for attempted assault," she said.

"Oh," I sighed. "How do you feel?"

"A bit relieved actually. Now he can be put away for some time so that I can sort out this mess. I also contacted my sheikh and told him everything and that I wanted a divorce."

"What did he say?"

"He was supportive but reminded me that there's an *iddah*, a period of time that we aren't allowed to have any physical contact, until he can go through with the divorce. So I'm waiting for that one..."

"Good for you," I rolled over on my stomach. "You deserve better. A pure soul should have pure love."

"Oh, I'm not that pure Ali," she murmured. "You have no idea how wicked I can be."

"I don't believe you Layla. You are a beautiful bird locked up in a cage. Soon that cage will be broken and you can be set free to drink the nectar of whatever flower you desire."

"You know Ali, there is such an intense love that no human can offer," she said.

"Have you felt it?"

"Yes, when my husband went to Iraq, I was all alone in my flat for forty days. I didn't meet anyone. I was just at home, by myself. I experienced such things..." she sighed.

"What did you experience?" I said.

"Him," she said.

"Him?" I said.

"Yes, him. I was standing on my prayer rug. I closed my eyes to find my focus before the prayer. I felt a pleasant breeze touching my face. I opened my eyes and saw a prayer rug in front of me. I saw him pass by me to go stand on the prayer rug. At first I was chocked. I couldn't believe that the man who everyone is looking for, waiting for, begging for, was standing in front of me. So many couplets, so many invocations, so many sighs and tears and wishes to meet the Imam of our time, yet he was here, with me. He initiated the prayer. I followed him. I couldn't raise my eyes, I was so absorbed in the prayer, in the presence, in the moment, that I became completely oblivious of my surrounding. *Everything* disappeared. My heart was racing. Tears flowed uncontrollably. I couldn't raise my head, it was as if the holiness of his presence was so grandeur that it didn't *allow* me to raise my head. I fell into such a trance that I was totally unaware of how he ended the prayer and left. I just remember his feet and the scent of jasmine that has followed me ever since. Even Masuma commented it the other day."

"Why are you telling me this?" I asked.

"Because I want you to know that even though everything feels so far away, he is closer than you think, he is present, beside you, but *you* are in *ghayba*, occultation, so you don't see him."

What she said made me think of the past. I'd done it all for him, to even the battle, to prepare for his coming, yet I had not thought of him for a second while doing it. I was so caught up in the action that I'd forgotten the very cause. It made me sad, but hopeful. Why had Layla contacted me in the first place? Why had our roads crossed? I started believing more and more that she was God sent to strengthen me on the path and connect me to the Imam. Did that mean that God saw me? That I had the attention of Imam Mahdi? Despite being so distracted?

"Thank you for telling me," I said after a moment.

"He is like the father that taught you how to bike, but don't forget to look back as you bike away on your adventures," she said.

Tears started to fall. I don't know why, but I felt heavy yet so empty at the same time.

"And when you fall, he is right there to pick you up again, caress your bruises and help you up again," she said.

I cried. She could probably hear me, but I didn't care.

"You know Ali, when you empty all the padding from the flute, that's when the melody is heard," she consoled.

"I just want to burn away in the sun, before I vanish in the darkness," I sobbed.

"The sun is shining dear, it is you who are clouded," she said.

Her words were like balm to my wounds.

"Why do you always make me cry?" I asked.

"I touch your soul," she said.

"How?"

"Because I just don't talk, I *speak*, speak with the soul. I am of the soul, from the soul, to the soul, and we will meet soon," she said cryptically and ended the call.

I was silent, absorbing the profound words that had rained on me. A text message woke me up from my thoughts.

> Oh you who are whole-bodily
> Undress

I smiled at Layla's cheeky style, and did what she said, literally. I undressed, pulled the sheets over me, closed my eyes and withdrew into the starry night.

I'd set all NSI members as VIP on my phone, meaning they could call through the "Do not disturb" mode and awaken me. Now one of those calls jumped me out of bed, my eyes dazzling from the morning rays. It was Fatima.

"Salam," she said. "We have a situation. I need you to listen carefully. Haji has been stopped at the gate for the Teheran departure. He is not officially under arrest but I doubt they will let him go any time soon. They will probably bypass standard custody rules and hold him more than three days as I believe the security police is involved. I'm acting as his attorney, but they're not giving much information. We are just about to walk into the interrogation room."

I knew what had to be done. And I knew that my dream was to be true.

11

The small room was gloomy gray. A basic set of table and chairs in white from IKEA. Johan Falkenberg was eyeing Haji, as he was eyeing him back. Dr. Mike Owens was sitting silently in the background observing.

"Do you know why you're here?" Falkenberg started.

"No," Haji said.

Falkenberg walked to one corner of the room and back. Haji followed him with his sight.

"Why do you have a USB drive with you?" Falkenberg tried.

"I didn't know it was illegal to bring USB drives on the flight." Haji snapped.

"Do you have any other USB drives?." Falkenberg said.

"Of course I do, like any other normal human being who lives in the 21st century. I have them in all of the colors of the rainbow," Haji sneered.

Falkenberg was unsure if it was an ironic reference to the Pride movement or just a figure of speech, so he let it pass. Better not to be distracted and stay focused on the main issue, he thought.

"Where are they?" Falkenberg said.

"At home," Haji said.

Falkenberg watched Owens and rolled his eyes.

"Can you tell me a bit about the contents of the USB drive? What are all these documents?" Owens said.

Haji faced Owens. "There are two books on the drive. I'm bringing them to Iran to publish them, to keep the price cost for each book low. As you might know, people are not fond of paying too much for litteratur. And even if they do, they obviously don't read so much."

Did he just sneer us again? Falkenberg thought.

Owens unbuttoned his sleeves and rolled them up. "What is 'The story of the Griffin' about?"

Haji stopped his mantra of "*la illaha ill Allah*" which he could perform without any lip movement. "Well Hafez has some stories in his *divan*, poetry collection, and some are selected in the book, with commentary.

"And what about 'Djinn exposed'?" Owens tried.

"It's about djinn and Satan, and how they confuse people in the world, like yourselves, who arrest and waste normal people's time based on false whispers. I highly recommend you to read it, there are some prescriptions on how to cure yourself as well," Haji snapped.

"You will have to stay in our custody until the USB drive has gone through forensics and all documents have been analyzed," Falkenberg resorted.

Fatima slammed the table. "You can't do that! What is your arresting order?"

"Threat towards national security," Falkenberg smirked. "We can do whatever we want."

Our Slack channel had turned into chaos. Everybody was panicking, suggesting all sorts of exaggerated ideas. "We should press charges," Jawad said. "We should demonstrate or even riot," Hassan countered. "We should go to the media," Hadi pleaded.

Hadi. I read his words with contempt, but it was better to let Haji deal with him.

"What are you talking about guys, this is the secret police, they bypass all of these society layers," I said.

"So what should we do Ali? Just sit and roll our thumbs? They got our leader!" Hadi jabbed.

"Just stay calm, he will be released within a day," I said.

"How do you know that? We can't trust your dreams on this," Khadija rebuked.

"I just know. If not, we can do whatever you want," I said, ignoring the comment regarding my dreams, but noted to not share everything with everyone again.

"Laqis! Why are the schematics not on the drive?!"

"I don't know, master," Laqis said.

"Where are they then?!"

"I don't know, master."

"Then what do you know you pathetic imbecille?! Why did I make you in charge of the Dark Forces? Get out of my sight, before I split you in half!"

Laqis left the meeting with a profound sense of perplexity. He summoned the core members of Dark Forces for a crisis meeting.

"Does Hajizadeh possess the schematics or not?" Laqis said.

"We don't know for sure master, but we don't think so."

"How can't we know for sure?" Laqis screamed.

"Because we can't penetrate Hajizadeh's heart. We have him under surveillance around the clock, but we can't even stay close to him. He is in constant *dhikr* so the scent that emanates from him resembles military degree smoke grenades."

"Have you approached him through any proxies?" Laqis said.

"Yes, the last proxy meeting we had was via Hadi. Hadi gave him the USB drive and he put it in his backpack, in front of Hadi. Hadi was with him the entire night and even drove Haijzadeh to the airport. The USB drive was never taken out hence the files should be there."

Laqis lost his temper. "Then how come they are not?! Didn't you verify that Ali copied the schematics to the drive, before handing it over to Hadi?!

"We did, master."

"So how can they have vanished from the drive by themselves?!" Laqis slammed.

"We don't know, master."

"Please, tell me at least you know what their next move is?!"

"I'm sorry, we don't..."

"Don't say..."

"...know master".

Laqis grabbed the back head of one of the soldiers, injected pure fear to his heart and slit out his throat. The soldier fell on his knees and then on his face, followed by the cracking sound of his skull as Laqis smashed it beneath his boots.

I entered the main entrance.

"Hi Dimitri," I said and had a long chat with the Russian janitor.

I picked up a latte macchiato, had a little chat with the barista and gave her a nice tip, so that she'll remember me.

Then I went to the auditorium where, ironically, the final exam in the network security course, was taking place. A good five hour exam, from 3 p.m. to

8 p.m. And I planned to stay until the last minute. I smiled, said *Bismillah*, opened the test and started writing.

Just before the 6 p.m. news report, the most popular news hour in Sweden, hell broke loose. All national media outlets reported it. Within the hour, it was broadcasted as breaking news, all over the world. The revolution had started.

Fatima stormed into the prosecutor's office and demanded Haji's immediate release.

"Given the latest news the so called threat to national security that my client is accused of posing is invalid. I hereby request that you release him or I will press charges against the security police for circumventing civil law. Also, I don't think SÄPO would be particularly fond of the news leaking to Aftonbladet, that a NSA officer is orchestrating a SÄPO operation, on Swedish land."

The prosecutor looked at Fatima. Her eyes were glowing with rage.

"One moment," he said, picked up the phone and briefed Johan Falkenberg.

"Yes sir, I will sir, ok sir," he said and ended the call.

"SÄPO no longer deems Mohsen Hajizadeh as a suspect and has no interest in holding him any further, so I will order his release. You may go now," the prosecutor said.

Fatima turned her heels and walked out of the room with a broad grin, leaving the door open.

"I don't understand," Falkenberg said. "We had Farooq Abdul-Aziz in custody, we had Mohsen Hajizadeh in custody, so how can this have happened? While they were in custody?!"

"I'm not sure," Owens said. "There must be a third person on the outside, helping them."

"I'm certain there's someone on the outside, but I don't believe he is connected to Abdul-Aziz or Hajizadeh. We have nothing, neither physical nor digital traces, that connect Abdul-Aziz to Hajizadeh. They have probably been framed in a larger operation. Where was the torrent published from?" Falkenberg asked.

"It was from the same computer on LTH, but this time a VPN tunnel was established to the computer from the Technion university in Israel, indicating that the computer has only been a host and not the actual origin," Owens said.

"That would free Abdul-Aziz from all charges," Falkenberg said.

"Yes," Owens said.

"Do you believe the Israelis are behind this operation?" Falkenberg said.

"The complexity and deception level surely

implies that," Owens said. "But there is a strong conflict of motive suggesting otherwise. It would be of the biggest disadvantage for the Israelis if F-18 technology got in the hands of their enemies."

"True that," Falkenberg said and looked out of the window with dismantling concern.

The time was past 10 p.m. when I finished the exam and arrived home. I surfed into The Pirate Bay and sorted torrents after popularity. The torrent containing the schematics for the F-18 was ranked first. During the four hours posted online, it had been seeded and downloaded over a million times, from IPs all over the world. From The Pirate Bay, it spread over to other torrent sites. YouTubers had already released in first analysis of the tech inside the documents. A multitude of different scenarios and applications were being discussed on a variety of Reddit sub forums. The news was even discussed on the notorious 4Chan forum, where anons were posting memes and gifs of everything, from how the US would hence forward, be dissected on the military scene, to how Somalian pirates would start looting air space as well. It started living its own life and it was impossible to delete it from the Internet now. I had scheduled the publishing just before going to the final exam, with such meticulous timing that it would never occur to the agents that it indeed had been scheduled at the perfect time, where all their current suspects and potential future suspects, including myself, had an alibi. And the *Ayn Ali* talisman had protected me from the radar of the Dark Forces.

By now the police had probably figured out that Stakkato's confiscated server was a connection hub. They will go through all user accounts on the machine. Anyone of the dussins of hackers will be among the potential suspects. But hackers are smart, they use aliases, they disguise their identities, even in trusted forums. Tracking down and investigating each one of them will take a horrendous amount of effort. And once they've done that and realized that they all were false leads, they will be baffled how Operation Griffin was pulled off. It couldn't be Stakkato because he was in custody, and stripped of his gear. The only one left is me, and I'm not listed as a user on Stakkato's server. I had originally helped Stakkato set up his connection hub, including setting the password for root and all other users. He hadn't granted me any access manually and we hadn't spoken in years since I moved to Malmö. I was fairly sure that he didn't even remember that I had access. And so, there was nothing left that connected me to Stakkato.

The idea of leaking the schematics on The Pirate

Bay wasn't something unplanned. The idea sparked years ago when I was sitting on the veranda with Haji, drinking a hot cup of ginger tea.

"I wish the world would be stripped of all modern weapons," I had said. "A world where wars and destinies were formed by such simple and equal rules, as bravery and tactics. Where one man had a more equal chance to make an impact. There are so many casualties today. A fourteen year old pimply kid sits behind the computer screen and drops a bomb from a drone as if it's a video game. Or the simple fact that weapons of mass destruction is what keeps the current power balance of the world, is totally absurd."

"Well, you cannot undue technology," said Haji. "Granted that the technology advancement have shaped the landscape of modern warfare, but from it many other technologies has emerged, that helps mankind as well."

"True," I said.

"However," Haji continued, taking a sip from his spicy tea, "what if we could even it out, a little bit?"

"How do you mean?" I said, noticing the sparkle in his eyes.

"Knowledge is for everyone, right?" Haji said. "So, what if we provided the forbidden knowledge to the sons of Adam? In the Biblical tradition, Adam was forbidden to eat from the tree of knowledge. Islam rejects this notion, how can knowledge be forbidden? Especially considering that the Qur'an states that God taught Adam the names of everything, so why would He then forbid His student from knowledge? It doesn't make sense. But the concept of forbidden knowledge is deeply integrated in capitalistic politics and economics. The idea of copyright and classified information are keystones to create monopolies and world domination. Innovations are held back due to copyrights, artists' creative spirits are inhibited and the masses are held in the dark, by what selected people in their government do; people who've been elected into office and granted power by the common citizens in the first place!"

"So, how do we change the status quo?" I asked.

"We might not be able to completely topple it, but at least we could make a dent," Haji said, and swept down the rest of the tea.

It was in that moment that the idea of Operation Griffin was born.

12

2 weeks later

Haji's living room looked the same. The glass cabinet with an ancient copy of the Persian poet Ferdowsi's magnum opus *Shahnameh*, the great painting of the typical Greek landscape with the white rectangular houses beside the blue ocean (Haji insisted though that it was Lebanon and not Greece), the dark U-shaped sofa around the TV, Fifa playing on the Playstation; here is where all the action happened, in the center of the house, amids all family chaos.

He poured me a mint drink, strong in flavor, with emerald hues and sweet as honey.

"Have you heard anything from Hadi?" I said.

Hadi had dropped a bomb on Slack last week. He wrote a three feet long post, describing how he felt suffocated by the group, how he couldn't express his artistic freedom and how fed up he was with everything.

Haji had replied with one sentence: "If I was such a bad leader, why did you not just talk to me, at least on that last day that you were with me, rather than informing on me?"

As Allamah Tabatabai writes, the heart is like a water tank, it needs to be cleansed before filled with water, otherwise the dirt will contaminate the water and eventually surface.

Hadi did not reply. He had no answer, really. He flew the day after to Hollywood to pursue the career he'd been promised, simultaneously ending his mission as a Nameless Soldier of the Imam.

"Forget him," Haji said. "He left us a long time ago, it just surfaced now. Let's look ahead, I have some plans in mind."

"Tell me more," I said.

"The group has been shaken by the latest happenings. On one hand, they cannot grasp the scope of what we've done and how we've done it, on the other hand they *now* realize that we have eyes on us. This is nothing new really, but for them it is. We need to strengthen them."

"How?" I said.

"We need to go to a camp," Haji said.

"Like the old days?" I said.

Memories of all the times we had gone to various camps flashed by. We rented a cabin somewhere in the Swedish forest, off grid, and had various spiritual exercises and discussions. It was simple in theory, to detach from the world and attach with the divine, but in practice, it was much harder. Not the detachment, apart from the time when Hassan was in charge of the food and bought only a bag of thin bread and cheese that was supposed to last for the entire weekend. "You said we were supposed to have the simple food of Imam Ali", Hassan cried when Haji jokingly rebuked him for trying to kill us by starvation. No, the challenge laid in maintaining the attachment to the divine when the camp was over and you returned home alone, surrounded by all temptations and distractions. Now that I thought of it, I really missed the retreats.

Haji took a sip from his mint drink. "Yes, but deeper, and longer. We need to go into the forest to lose our minds and find our souls. When we break the shackles of worldly comfort, we will soar to new spiritual heights. There are some things I need to say, that I can only do by the camp fire, by looking into their eyes, by touching their souls with my own. Under the full moon, give them a glimpse of the mysteries behind all of this."

"Do you think they have doubts?" I said.

"No," Haji said. "I don't think, I know. We need to remove it, we need to show them what we see."

"Laqis, these covert operations of yours are not working."

"Yes master," Laqis said, shame covering his downcast face.

113

"We have lost an important battle, but we cannot lose the war."

"Of course, master," Laqis said.

"I want you to re-organize the Dark Forces, and leave the covert operations."

"Do you mean..."

"Yes. Full scale war, in broad daylight, under the visible sun."

"But my soldiers neither have the strength nor training for that type of warfare," Laqis said.

"They will from this day on. I have summoned two of the djinn from the well of B'er Dhat al-Ilm in the valley of Kathib Azraq."

"Are they not from the djinn who revolted against Sulayman ibn Dawood?" Laqis said.

"Yes. Many armies who have passed the valley and neared the well for water have been slain by them. They didn't even spare the milk brother of Mohammad ibn Abdullah who was sent to bring water, for Muslims, camping nearby."

"That's just what we need master," Laqis said.

"They will join your forces and are not hesitant to expose themselves to humans. Gather the intel and manipulate the scene as you always do, but this time don't send any proxies, send them to execute the bloody finale instead."

"Yes, master!" Laqis said and left the meeting with an evil grin.

On the train back to Malmö, I received a call from Layla.

"So, I never had the chance to meet you," I said.

"I'm sorry for that, Ali. I had to go back to follow up on the divorce," she said with that hoarse voice of hers. "But guess what?"

"What?"

"I will get to meet the greatest *aref*, mystic, of Europe!" she said.

"God, that sounds incredible, how come?" I said.

"Well he is the head of the Islamic Center and is appointed as responsible for entire Europe. He heard about my family situation and also about my spiritual journey and some of the things I've witnessed, and he liked to meet me in person," she said.

"That's great news," I said, trying hard not to let that sudden queasy feeling leak into my voice. Was it jealousy? Where did it come from? And why did I feel that?

"I will let you know how it goes," she said. "Thank you, for everything Ali, really, I mean it. Because of you I dared to break the cage and be set myself free. No woman deserves to live under oppression, no one, and I'm sad that many men don't understand that, but you truly do and for that I admire you, your kind heart and pure love."

"I don't know what to say." She always touched my heart in the most profound yet unexpected way.

"You don't need to say anything dear, just absorb and blossom," she said and ended the call, leaving me with a bittersweet feeling.

My feelings had not yet settled when I arrived in Malmö. Nora met me up and wanted to talk. We went to the Espresso House, by the central square. It had such a cozy interior and the chai latte was exceptionally sweet.

"I finally did it," Nora exclaimed.

"Great! What did you do?" I took a sip from my chai.

"Bought tickets," she said. "To Marocco."

"To Marocco?" I said. "To meet your..."

"Dad, yeah. At last, I found the courage to do it," she beamed.

"How?" I asked.

"In you."

"In me?"

"Yes, your acts of bravery the last weeks. How you stood up for a total stranger, how you met a pack of wolves without so much as hesitating. That made me think, can't I stand up for my own father? And against whom? My own mother, not an enemy that wants to hurt me." There was a warmness in her smile.

"What did your mother say?"

"That's the most ironic part! She was proud! I told her I wanted to find my roots to shape my identity. I explained that I understood the painful memories she bore but I remembered them differently. And even though my father was the worst husband, it didn't change the fact that he was the best dad, at least from the perspective of a child."

I smiled at her. Her eyes were sparkling as she spoke.

"She kissed me and we hugged each other. She said that I've grown up and become an adult and that from now on I had to make my own decisions, wise choices and mistakes. That was the course of life, and I had her blessing."

"How long will you be gone?" I asked.

"A month."

"Wow, that's long," I sighed.

"Will you miss me?" Her big green eyes sought mine.

We looked at each other. When eyes truly meet, there is either fire or ice, the condition of the heart. We were not married, we were not engaged, I honestly didn't know what we were, as we strolled along the borders of "it's complicated". I didn't want to break her heart, or even make her a tiny bit sad, so I let her tide carry me along.

"I will," I reassured. "But you go find your answers and come back and we'll have a serious talk."

"About what?" she asked, looking deep into my eyes. I felt her flames, now was the moment to break free from the stream or drift away into the sea.

"If your father indeed is the Hulk or not, and hence if you are the She-Hulk or not," I said.

"How will that change things?" she exclaimed.

"Well, if you are of Hulk blood, Marvel will create all sorts of juridical problems pertaining copyright, if I recruit you to the DC Universe and Justice League," I said, sounding way more serious than anticipated.

"Oh, so you want me in your team, Mr Behrooz Wayne?" she teased.

"I'm not sure," I said, clenching my fingers. "Firstly, Wonder Woman would be jealous and I wouldn't want any drama. Secondly, I don't know if a rage machine would operate well under the command of a tactical perfectionist. However, what would be the fun of a world with total order and no chaos?"

"Sounds a lot like love to me," she said.

"It does," I said. "It does, indeed."

GLOSSARY

Alhamdulillah - Praise and thanks be to God.

Azan - Call to prayers.

Bismillah - "In the name of God", usually said before eating food or doing some good deeds.

Bismillah Rahman Rahim - "In the name of God the Beneficent the Merciful", a common phrase recited before performing many tasks, such as worship or eating.

Dhikr - Divine mantra where you repeat holy words such as God's various names.

Djinn - Invisible species created from smokeless fire, the evil among them commonly known as demons. Satan is a djinn.

Fajr - Dawn prayer.

Fatwa - Religious decree. Example: "Pig meat is forbidden to eat".

Fiqh - Religious jurisprudence, more specifically laws pertaining Islam. For example what is allowed or forbidden to eat, laws pertaining fasting, rules for prayers etc.

Hadith - A reported saying of Prophet Mohammad.

Hasbunallah wa n'emal wakil - "God is sufficient and the best advocate".

Iddah - A period of time, around two-three months, that a husband and wife, who wants to divorce, aren't allowed to have intercourse, so the divorce can be fulfilled.

Irfan - Islamic mysticism and spirituality.

Istighfar - Asking God for forgiveness.

Jihad - "Struggle", used physically to denote military resistance and self-defense, and spiritually as a struggle against one's selfish desires.

Karamat - Miracles.

La illaha ill Allah - "There is no God but Allah".

Salawat - Sending blessings and peace on Prophet Mohammad and his family.

Seyyed - Direct descendant of Prophet Mohammad. If he is an Islamic priest, his turban is black denoting his lineage.

Sheikh - Islamic priest, wearing a white turban.

Shalwar-qamis - Type of clothes usually worn in Pakistan-Afghanistan area consisting of a longer shirt reaching the knees, and pants.

Sirat - The straight path in this life, and the straight bridge over Hell that leads to Paradise in the next life.

SobhanAllah - "Glory be to God", like an Islamic version of Halleluja.

Sujood - Prostrating on the ground, i.e. having the forehead on the ground in worship.

Sunnah - Traditions and customs of Prophet Mohammad.

Takbir - Saying "Allahu Akbar" - God is greater.

Tawfiq - God's granting of success or possibility to do something.

Ulema - Plural for "alem" - Islamic scholar.

Urefa - Plural for "aref" - mystic (a practiser of Irfan).

Wodho - Ritual washing for prayers.

Zohoor - When Imam Mahdi appears at the End of Times to cleanse the world from evil and injustice.

www.ingramcontent.com/pod-product-compliance
Lightning Source LLC
Chambersburg PA
CBHW030314130626
46549CB00002B/843